BAROQUE AT DAWN

OTHER BOOKS BY NICOLE BROSSARD
IN ENGLISH TRANSLATION

A Book (1976, novel),
translated by Larry Shouldice

Turn of a Pang (1976, novel),
translated by Patricia Claxton

Daydream Mechanics (1980, poetry),
translated by Larry Shouldice

These Our Mothers (1983, theoretical fiction),
translated by Barbara Godard

French Kiss (1986, novel),
translated by Patricia Claxton

Lovhers (1986, poetry),
translated by Barbara Godard

The Aerial Letter (1988, essays),
translated by Marlene Wildeman

Surfaces of Sense (1989, novel),
translated by Fiona Strachan

Mauve Desert (1990, novel),
translated by Susanne de Lotbinière-Harwood

Picture Theory (1991, novel),
translated by Barbara Godard

BAROQUE AT DAWN

NICOLE BROSSARD

TRANSLATED BY PATRICIA CLAXTON

Originally published as *Baroque d'aube* by Éditions de l'Hexagone

Canadian Cataloguing in Publication Data

Brossard, Nicole, 1943–
    [Baroque d'aube. English]
    Baroque at dawn

Translation of Baroque d'aube.

ISBN 0-7710-1684-0

I. Claxton, Patricia, 1929– .   II. Title.   III. Title: Baroque d'aube.
English.

PS8503.R7B3713   1997   C843'.54   C97-930555-1

The translation of the text was completed with the support of the
Canada Council.

The publishers acknowledge the support of the Canada Council and
the Ontario Arts Council for their publishing program.

Typesetting by IBEX Graphic Communications Inc.
Printed and bound in Canada

McClelland & Stewart Inc.
The Canadian Publishers
481 University Avenue
Toronto, Ontario
M5G 2E9

1 2 3 4 5   01 00 99 98 97

"I shall not recount my reasoning."

— SAMUEL BECKETT

HOTEL RAFALE

"What I want is to celebrate the woman who owns my shadow; she who rescues names and faces from obscurity."

— ALEJANDRA PIZARNIK

First the dawn. Then the woman came.

In Room 43 at the Hotel Rafale, in the heart of a North American city armed to the teeth, in the heart of a civilization of gangs, artists, dreams and computers, in darkness so complete it swallowed all countries, Cybil Noland lay between the legs of a woman she had met just a few hours before. For a time which seemed a coon's age and very nocturnal, the woman had repeated, "Devastate me, eat me up." Cybil Noland had plied her tongue with redoubled ardour and finally heard, "Day, vastate me, heat me up." The woman's thighs trembled slightly and then her body orbited the planet as if the pleasure in her had transformed to a stupendous aerial life reflex.

Cybil Noland had felt the sea enter her thoughts like a rhyme, a kind of sonnet which briefly brought her close to Louise Labé, then drew away to pound elsewhere, wave sounds in present tense. The sea had penetrated her while whispering livable phrases in her ear, drawn-out laments, a lifelong habit with its thousand double exposures of light. Later, thoughts of the sea cast her against a boundless wall of questions.

~

In the room, the air conditioner is making an infernal noise. Dawn has given signs of life. Cybil can now make out the furniture shapes and see, reflected in the mirror on the half-open bathroom door, a chair on which are draped a blue T-shirt, a pair of jeans and a black leather jacket. On the rug, a pair of sandals one beside the other.

The woman puts a hand on Cybil Noland's hair, the other touching a shoulder. The stranger at rest is terribly alive, anonymous with her thousand identities in repose. Cybil Noland turns so as to rest her cheek comfortably in the curve of the other's crotch. Neither thinks to move, much less to talk. Each is from somewhere else, each is elsewhere in her life of elsewhere, as if living some life from the past.

~

Cybil Noland had travelled a lot, to cities with light-filled curves shimmering with headlights and neon signs. She loved suspense, the kind of risk that might now take as simple a guise as strolling about among the buildings of big cities. She had always declined to stay in the mountains or the country or beside a lake, even for a few days. Her past life had unfolded at a city pace, in the presence of many accents, traffic sounds and speed, all of which sharpen the senses. Over the years she had come to love sunsets reddened by carbon dioxide. It had been so long since she had seen the stars that the names of the constellations had long ago vanished into her memory's recesses. Cybil Noland lived at information's pace. Information was her firmament, her inner sea, her Everest, her cosmos. She loved the electric sensation she felt at the speed of passing images. Each image was easy. It was easy for her to forget what it was that had excited her a moment before. Sometimes she thought she ought to resist this frenetic consumption of words, catastrophes, speed, rumours, fears and screens, but too late, her intoxication seemed irreversible. Between fifteen and thirty years of age she had studied history, literature and the curious laws that govern life's instinct for continuation. Thus she had learned to navigate among beliefs and dreams dispersed over generations and centuries. But today all that seemed far away, ill-suited to the speed with which reality was spinning out her anxiety with its sequences of happiness and violence, its fiction grafted like a science to the heart of instinct. As a child she had learned several languages, enabling her today to consume twice the information, commentary, tragedy, minor mishaps and prognostications. Thus she had unwittingly acquired a taste for glib words and fleeting images. All she had learned in her youth finally came to seem merely muddleheaded, anachronistic and obsolete.

On this July night that was drawing to a close in a small hotel in a city armed to the teeth, Cybil Noland had felt the sea rise up and swallow her. Something had spilled over, creating a vivid horizontal effect, but simultaneously a barrier of questions. The sky, the stars and the sea had synthesized an entire civilization of cities in her when the woman came.

There between the stranger's legs, questions arose, insistent, intrusive questions, snooping questions, basic questions seeking alternately to confirm and deny the world and its raison d'être. Borne on this current of questions, Cybil Noland vowed to renounce glib pronouncements without however willingly foregoing the dangerous euphoria elicited by the fast, frenzied images of her century.

～

The light was now diffused throughout the room, a yellow morning light which in movies of yesteryear gave the dialogue a hopeful turn, for the simple reason that mornings in those days were slow with the natural slowness that suited the movements made by heroines when, upon awakening, they gracefully stretched their arms, raising arches of carnal triumph in the air.

The woman has moved her legs to change position, perhaps to leave the bed. Cybil Noland has raised her head then her body in such fashion as to hoist herself up to the level of the woman's face. The mattress is uncomfortable, with hollows and soft spots one's elbows and knees sink into.

Since meeting, the two have barely exchanged three sentences. The woman is a musician and young. "*But I'm not sixteen,*" she said with a smile in the elevator. Cybil Noland thereupon nicknamed her "La Sixtine." On arrival in the room, they undressed and the woman ordered, "Eat me."

Now that Cybil Noland has the woman's living face at eye level, her belly swells again rich with desire like a tempestuous wind. *Kiss me, kiss m'again.*[1] With fire and festivity in her eyes, the woman looks Cybil over, caresses her, then thrusts her tongue between her lips. It might have been just a kiss, but what a way she has of breathing, of pearling each lip, tracing *abc* inside Cybil's mouth with the tiniest movements, impossible to separate the letters *abc*, to stop, demon delirium *abc* a constellation of flavours in her mouth. Then the wind surges, sweeping eyelashes, drying the perspiration about the neck, smoothing silken cheeks, closing eyelids, imprinting the outlines of faces deep in the pillow. The five sibyls of the Sixtine Chapel orbit the planet and the questions return. Cybil Noland opens her eyes. There are still traces of mascara on the woman's eyelashes. She too unseals her eyes. The look they give is laughing, languid, offering an intimacy glimpsable only in the strictest anonymity. Like a love-crazed thing all of a sudden, Cybil is aburn for this anonymous woman who had caught her eye in the bar of the Hotel Rafale. Something is exciting her, something about the anonymity of this woman encountered in the middle of a huge city, something that says, I don't know your name but I recognize the smooth curvaceous shape your body takes when navigating to the open sea. Soon I shall know where your tears, your savage words and anxious gestures hide, the things that will lead me to divine everything about you at one fell swoop. Thus does imagination take us beyond the visible, propelling us toward new faces that will set the wind asurge despite the barrier formed by vertical cities, despite the speed of life that drains our thoughts and leaves them indolent. The priceless eyes of desire are right to succumb to seduction so that one's familiar, everyday body may find joy in the thousands of anonymous others encountered along the way, bodies pursuing their destinies in cities saturated with feelings and emotions.

◦

The stranger gives off a scent of complex life which coils about Cybil Noland. City smells clinging to her hair like a social ego; fragrant, singularizing sandalwood, a trace of navel salt, the milky taste of her breasts. Everywhere an infiltration of life, aromatic, while the child in one does the rounds of all the smells, anonymously like a grown-up in a hurry to get thinking.

The air conditioner has stopped. There's silence. A surprising silence like the heady smell of lilac when the month of May reaches us at the exits of great, sense-deadening cages of glass and concrete. The silence draws out, palpable and appealing like La Sixtine's body. The alarm-clock dial on the bedside table is blinking. A power failure. Which means unbearable heat in exchange for a silence rare and more precious than gold and caviar. The silence is now diffused throughout the room. Surprising, devastating. An unreal silence that's terribly alive, as if imposing a kind of fiction by turning the eyes of the heart toward an unfathomable inner life.

The women lie side by side, legs entwined and each with an arm under the other's neck like sleepy reflex arcs. Suddenly Cybil Noland can stand no more of this new silence that has come and imposed itself on top of the first, which had been a silence tacitly agreed between them like a stylized modesty, an elegant discretion, a kind of meditative state capable of shutting out the sounds of civilization and creating a fictional time favourable to the appearance of each one's essential face.

⌁

Cybil Noland had brought the woman up to her room thinking of what she called each woman's essential face in her own destiny. Each time she had sex with a woman, this was what put heart into her desire. She was ready for anything, any kind of caress, any and all sexual scenarios, aware that you can never foresee exactly when, or for how long, an orgasm will recompose the lines of the mouth and chin, make the eyelids droop, dilate the pupils or keep the eyes shining. Most often the face would describe its own aura of ecstasy, beginning with the light filtering through the enigmatic slit between the eyelids when they hover half-closed halfway between life and pleasure. Then would come the split second that changed the iris into the shape of a crescent moon, before the white of the eye, whiter than the soul, proliferated multiples of the word imagery deep in her thoughts. This was how a woman who moments earlier had been a total stranger became a loved one capable of changing the course of time for the better.

All, thought Cybil Noland, so that the essential face that shows what women are really capable of may be seen, vulnerable and radiant, infinitely human, desperately disturbing. But for this to happen, the whole sea would have to flood into her mouth, and the wind flatten her hair to her skull, and fire ignite from fire, and she would have to consider everything very carefully at the speed of life and wait for the woman to possess her own silence, out of breath and beyond words in the midst of her present. In the well of her pleasure the woman would have to find her own space, a place of choice.

So when the air conditioner stopped, Cybil Noland felt she had been robbed of the rare and singular silence that had brought her so close to La Sixtine. As if she had suddenly realized that while the words *heat me vast*[2] were ringing with their thousand possibilities and her delicate tongue was separating the lips of La Sixtine's sex, civilization had nevertheless continued its headlong course.

Now the new silence is crowding the silence that accompanies one's most private thoughts. While groping for a comparison to explain this new silence, suddenly Cybil Noland can stand no more of it and wants to speak, will speak, but the woman comes close and reclines on top of her and with her warm belly and hair tickling Cybil's nose, and breasts brushing over Cybil's mouth, seems determined to turn Cybil's body into an object of pure erotic pleasure.

You'd say she was going. To say. Yes, she murmurs inarticulate sounds in Cybil's ear, rhythms, senseless words, catches her breath, plays on it momentarily, "That good?" she breathes. "That better?" Then over Cybil's body strews images and succulent words that burst in the mouth like berries. Now her sounds caress like violins. The names of constellations come suddenly to Cybil's mind: Draco the Dragon, Coma Berenices, Cassiopaeia and Lyra for the Northern Hemisphere; Sculptor, Tucana, Apus the Bird of Paradise, Ara the Altar for the Southern. Then the whole sea spreads through her and La Sixtine relaxes her hold.

~

You'd say she was going to tell a story. Something with the word joyous in the sentence to go with her nakedness there in the middle of the room. Once she's in the shower the water runs hard. She sings. When she lifts her tongue the sounds crowd up from under, full of vim. Joyously her voice spews out, zigzags from one word to another, cheerily penetrating Cybil Noland's consciousness as she lies half asleep in the spacious bed.

"I'll tell you a story," La Sixtine said, opening the window before getting in the shower. The window opens onto a fire escape. The curtain moves gently. Cybil Noland watches the movements of the fish, seaweed and coral in the curtain's design. Life is a backdrop against which thoughts and memories overlap. Life moves ever so slightly, goes through static stages, skews off, brings its humanism to the midst of armed cities like a provocation, a paradox that makes you smile. In spite of yourself. The dark fish throw a shadow over the pinks and whites of the coral, Cybil Noland thinks before riding off again, a deep-sea wanderer aboard great incunabula.

∾

The power's back on. The air conditioner's working. In the corridor, the chambermaids are bustling back and forth again.

When she got out of the shower La Sixtine turned on the radio. A sombre voice entered the room, spreading a smell of war and filth. The voice waded its way through "today the authorities" and "many bodies in front of the cathedral, some horribly mutilated. Foetuses were seen hanging from the gutted bellies of their mothers. In places the snow seemed coated with blood. Old women, open-mouthed and staring toward the cold infinity of the region leading to the sea, spoke of human limbs scattered about the ground. Other witnesses talked of hearing the cries of children although no children have been found. At present the authorities are unable to say what group the dead belong to since from their clothing one cannot tell whether they are from the north-east or the east-north."

One after another the sentences fall to the room's pink carpet. Cybil Noland watches from the spacious bed. La Sixtine sits on the edge of the bed with a towel about her hips and seems to be breathing with difficulty. Then, as if tired of trying to find her breath, she turns and curls her body into Cybil's trembling nakedness. Her head weighs heavily. Her body is heavy. The present is a body. The body is a live, pure present that goes on forever between the electrical thrum of the air conditioner and the voice from the radio.

Cybil Noland thinks about the morning she spent in a Covent Garden café. Her head that morning was full of a woman who wants to write a novel. This woman lacks vocabulary to describe the volcano of violence erupting in cities. She is sitting in a large kitchen. While she spoons sugar into her teacup with a little silver spoon, her hair brushes over the sugar bowl. She is young and resolute, in contrast with the fact that she is still in pyjamas at this late morning hour. There is a dictionary on the table. With one hand she holds the silver spoon and with the other absent-mindedly turns the pages of the dictionary. She gets up and goes to the window, where for a minute she leans on the sill. From here she can see the approaches to Hyde

Park, the texture of the day and the fine rain of this weather that penetrates the very core of one. She gazes into the distance. At the far side of herself, she ponders a fictional life. She observes so meticulously that the pondering fits her head and thoughts like a helmet. A book by Samuel Beckett lies on the table. The sugar bowl looks like a volcano. The woman lives alone, surrounded by ferns and a wealth of other plants to which she will put no names so that in their green anonymity they will create a fine, rich tropical forest for her. The rain falls slowly. She lights a cigarette. Why would she write this violent book? She has no special gift for it, or vocabulary or experience. She puts a hand on the dictionary and draws it close. The hand stays resting on the cover as though she's about to take an oath. With the other hand she writes a list of violent words, words that turn one's stomach, turn one's head to suffering, to people and their progeny who thirst for vengeance. Beyond the window Hyde Park glows, adding to its mystery, offering its trees and green lawns as so many hypotheses that liven vertigo in contemplation of the future. Truth will never come without worry, nor will the illusion of truth. The woman pours herself another cup of tea. Her father's oak-panelled library is filled with women's books. Her father's books are stacked in the north corner of the kitchen. They stand there like three Towers of Babel. Three towers of leather-bound volumes showing their gold-leafed spines.

The fine rain keeps falling and the woman treasures those images of the north that make her homesick. It isn't memory that does it, it's this taste of happiness split in two by silence.

⋄

In the room at the Hotel Rafale the solemn voice rustled
about like a small reptile, listing the incidences of violence that had marked the previous day. La Sixtine's
body was aquiver with all of humanity's futile present
and Cybil Noland no longer knew how or where to
touch her. She sought to catch La Sixtine's eye but could
not. The other's eyes were fixed on words as obstacles.
The solemn voice could not go on talking about death
for ever and Cybil kept waiting for the wrap-up, confident that then La Sixtine would abandon this terribly
awkward, limb-numbing *pietà* pose. But the voice kept
talking. Death was coming from every side, racing down
from north to south, erasing the planet from west to
east, advancing on the living with a reassuring patriar-
chal air, then at a single stroke disseminating its logic
and other deathly instruments in phalanx and phallus
form. Death came supreme, media-borne, into the spacious bed while in her head and thoughts Cybil Noland
clung to a passion for life as to a fine cliché, the kind on
which hope so loves to feed.

⋄

The Hyde Park woman reappears. The Samuel Beckett
book, a curiosity, lies between a bowl of fruit and the
corner window. The rain is audible. The woman is
writing, and in Cybil's mind this should be enough to
silence the portentous voice. Finally a calypso tune
effaces all disasters. La Sixtine takes the opportunity to

get up and slip on her panties, asking as she does where Cybil is from and what has brought her to this city. Cybil says it's not good to talk on an empty stomach and through dry lips and dials the desk to order up something to eat and drink. Then she takes her turn in the shower and the comfort of the water, and is soon absorbed in a bottomless reverie in which each cell of her flesh and fancy glows warm and bountifully. Caught up in the play of imprecise words and fuzzy thoughts, she swims with surprising vigour among the ribbonfish and salpas and lantern fish of the twilight zone. Watery metaphors file by. Now and then she slows her pace to admire the shapes and surprisingly bright colours here between the light-saturated blue so to speak and the blue-black of the unchangeable abyss. Then the strong ocean currents become a fine rain that makes her think of Scotland and paradoxically of the softness of a great many French words. When she opens her eyes there are two or three drops of water glistening under the showerhead.

She has barely emerged from the bathroom before La Sixtine asks with a touch of concern in her voice whether she's in the habit of "taking the elevator" with perfect strangers. The answer crackles.

"If possible, yes. I like the sea sounds made by stranger-women when they caress and allow themselves to make love beyond all conventional limits. Ah yes, I'm fasci-nated by the mind's strange process that requires the body to carry out an instant synthesis of two desires, the other's and one's own. In the sexual meeting of two stranger-women there's a temporal break that allows abstraction of the background baggage carried by each. Less of the past benefits an immediate presence."

"Yes but what's the good of immediate presence if it stays caged up in anonymity?"

"It makes one more aware. It allows you freedom of movement in time, lets you fly high or low and use that marvellous capacity we have of producing sense with our senses. Perhaps too it sets you burning amid the questions, lets you see the universe as an alibi for our hybrid desires afire to see some landscape. Perhaps."

La Sixtine did not understand all of Cybil Noland's passionate pronouncement but she liked having to wonder about the mysterious things the stranger was talking about. In any event, she was enjoying Cybil's voice and perfume and gesturing. She pressed for more.

"So how am I different from other women you've met through the luck of a city's draw?"

"The city, the hotel, this room, how we met – all of this means you're no longer anonymous for me. I don't think I need to go over every last little thing that makes us happy."

"What part am I going to play in your memory when you've left this city? Aren't you interested at all in me, my story, the part of me that was there before we met?"

"Isn't it the same for you about me? What would you do with my story if I told it to you?"

"I'd make a new one of it. I'd use it to increase my chances of having such rich and contradictory feelings for you that I'd never be able to leave you."

"I think you'd incorporate my story in your own by fabulating around a few very ordinary words and deeds. You'd make up a me, I'm sure of it."

"Maybe, and what's wrong with that?"

"Nothing, but don't pretend you want to know *me*."

"Nobody exists outside her own story – admit it."

"You need more than a story if you're going to understand people. I mean, to know where you stand with them.

"Knowing the other means becoming part of her story."

"You're wrong. Knowing the other means being able to fill in her story as she would tell it."

"When I say what I'm saying I'm not trying to break down your resistance to anything that sounds biographical. Where do we get our incorrigible yen to be part of whatever it is in the other that makes for memories and dreams?

"It's a matter of nose partly, always wanting to know the other's story as we do. Sniffing the other out. Comparing. Never feeling alone."

La Sixtine tucked an imaginary violin under her chin. "Would you like me to play you my life?"

There was such gentleness in the question that Cybil could not refuse. So, with uncharacteristic shyness, La Sixtine sat down at a respectable distance from Cybil and told her story.

∾

She began with her maternal grandparents, who seemed to have spent their lives partying and revelling under the palms and orange trees of Los Angeles. With each sentence she associated Paula and Robert's youth with the warm, fragrant pathways skirting the grounds of their first bungalow. Paula was an actress. Robert was a portrait photographer. For many years he captured the look in Hollywood actors' eyes – nostalgic eyes, drunkards', seducers' and divas' eyes, revealing ambition, intelligence or emptiness. And the look in each set of eyes was played out, accrued in value amid screenplays and first nights. And so all through his life Robert had witnessed first-hand the triumphs and tragedies that had moulded the features of three generations of men and women who made a joke of the celebrity-worship destined to shape a part of the psyche of North America.

Paula was born in Texas and Robert had come from the French province of Canada, the country north of the United States, the land of snows and dark Novembers. With the years, Robert had lost his mother tongue, although he had kept a small vocabulary that served him exclusively on nights of champagne, revelry and amorous frolic, when he would repeat voraciously to Paula before penetrating her, "*Ah! Ma belle créature.*" When their daughter Jeanne was born, Paula was already famous and Robert had begun to look like the men in his photographs. Jeanne grew up amid housemaids and cocktail parties. When she was twenty she met a young soldier by the name of James Kreig. "My parents were married in a little church in Santa Monica and for their honeymoon went to Quebec City, my grandfather's home town. My mother always regretted this trip in the middle of winter to a city that was like a set for the movie *I Confess*. My father rose quickly through the ranks of the army and after a few years was promoted to general. My mother was utterly devoted to him.

"It's mysterious how a man and woman can become so close. How gestures, though originally devised to separate men and women, come to be understood as companionable signs capable of kindling quixotic erotic affection.

"There was a Sunday afternoon I remember well. My father was reading and my mother was getting ready to go to a friend's house for tea. She was pulling on long white gloves while talking to him about what time she would probably be back. She came close and kissed him

on the neck where a soldier's hair is no longer than a
two-day beard. He bent his head to that side as if to hold
the kiss and its fragrance between his cheek and his
shoulder. His right hand brushed my mother's dress. I've
always been intrigued by these simple, familiar gestures.
How can two bodies at first totally unknown to each
other come to blend their secret smells so that no one
around them can thereafter penetrate that invisible wall
we call intimacy? How do the manias, messages, man-
nerisms, fixations and fancies brought by each and
melded create the cultural microclimate that makes a
couple's or family's relationship?"

La Sixtine denied herself no artifice when speaking. She
played her words the way one plays a trout in springtime.

"Imagine my mother vowing as she married to be as
perfect as her soldier. Imagine for a moment that perfection in her voice and gestures. And the cleanliness of
each of the houses I grew up in. Four years in Paris, three
in Manila, a year in Saigon, two years in Baden-Baden
and seven in Latin America. Imagine my mother giving
her orders to the maids and menservants. Imagine their
deference, diligence and courtesy. Imagine how they
lived. And now look at me. I'm six. I'm wearing a white
taffeta frock. I'm standing in a big room and stifling
heat. There's a piano, plants, a fuschia sofa and a big
bamboo chair. You can hear the hum of a fan over my
head. My teacher is a shy, sad, dreamy young man who
smells of Old Spice. The violin is heavy, like an uncontrollable albatross. My fingers are moist and slip on the

rough strings. The bow is like a little sword. In the privacy of my own room, I lay it ceremoniously on my shoulder and declare myself a Knight of the Table of Harmony. I am a child and in my games I shout and sing. Sometimes I point my sword at the sky and threaten God. Despite the unbearable heat and the instrument's recalcitrance, I know I'm going to be a violinist. My head full of this fine purpose, I will have the best of thoughts along with the sounds both deep and high-pitched about to leap from the table of harmony.

"When I turned sixteen the family had been living in Buenos Aires for two years. My talent was already being praised in ambassadorial circles, where I would play a little melancholia from time to time. One day, during discussion of a big benefit evening which all Buenos Aires would be attending, the beautiful wife of an admiral suggested that I should accompany Ismelda Rubi, the renowned tango singer. 'It would be so different, two women playing the most beautiful tangos of Buenos Aires,' she said, gazing straight into my eyes as though I were the seventh wonder of the world. That's how the tango came into my life. By a woman's will and whim.

"I saw the admiral's wife quite a few times more. My mother kept praising her beauty and my father admired the elegance she displayed when talking about music or the great painters or literature. So when she suggested to my parents that she take me to see *Madame Butterfly* at the Teatro Colón, they were simply enchanted. This woman could well complete my education, they thought.

"I liked being with the woman, who treated me like an adult. That she could converse with an adolescent about Leonardo da Vinci, Marie Curie and Jorge Luis Borges was proof of intelligence and sensitivity and made me look up to her.

"The months went by and we went to the opera several times. Amid all these splendours, I imagined the life she must have led. Often she would turn to me and whisper a few words, to which I would nod agreement, for watching the performance beside her was always a source of contentment for me. Her perfume created an aura above our heads. When she crossed her legs the friction of nylon against nylon drew my eyes down to her knees.

"Sometimes after the opera she would ask the driver to wait for us for an hour, perhaps two according to her impulse of the moment. Most often we would go and walk on Corrientes Avenue. She would take my arm and I would feel her hand near my breast. Sometimes we had to walk sideways to thread our way through the dense crowd. These places delighted me and I loved stopping for a pastry or something to drink. We would go into every bookstore we passed. If I picked up a book to leaf through, she would come up behind me and read over my shoulder with such intensity that I would imagine her heat reaching my back knotlike then branching upward into my neck.

"There were evenings when the driver would take us to the far side of the city. The car would stop. Hotel

Alvear. There, she would order champagne and hold my hand, gazing nostalgically ahead of her. Each time, she would ask me if I wanted to be a composer. Each time I would reply, 'I don't know. Still.' The palm of her hand would rest lightly on my finger joints and I felt that the softness of her skin could protect me to my bones against the inclemencies of the world. A pocket of warm air formed between her palm and my finger joints and remained there between her thoughts and mine, a hanging garden filled with fruits and their scent. When she talked she liked to begin each sentence with 'before' or 'after,' as if there had been two distinct periods in her life. I don't really know by what wiles of language, but she had only to pronounce a few sentences and I was in a surrealistic other world. But there were evenings when there was nothing festive in her eyes. Methodically and precisely, she recounted in chronological order the events of what she called 'the history of the evil.' Once established in words, she said, the evil was empowered to circulate unimpeded. On those evenings the words fell from her mouth with such authority that one would have thought it within her power to efface untruth and distrust forever from this planet. '*Machismo* leaves deep cavities in women's hearts,' she said, 'and each cavity must be filled with women's tears. When the women have no tears left their daughters take their place; then the daughters bend their heads over the cavities so as to fill them with their laments.' On other evenings she would talk of a little girl alone beside the sea. The little girl had made a mermaid and a starfish of fine sand. The sea had washed them away.

"One day after we had lunched together in La Recoleta, the admiral's wife wanted to take me to see her mother's grave.

"We are walking between the burial vaults. It's very hot. The cemetery is deserted at this hour. Now and then there are flowers at the foot of a grave, petals, tools lying about, a bucket of lime. We stop often to read the inscriptions or to touch a madonna or an angel's face engraved in the marble. At each stop she tells a story. Sometimes she gets ahead of me and bends to read the inscription, then turns to me, waiting impatiently for me to come and hear her tale of long-gone, historically questionable facts as far away as Patagonia. Her enthusiasm never flags from one grave to the next. Soon we come to the tomb of Eva Perón, about whom she says not a word, recalling instead the Sundays of her childhood and other even happier Sundays when one could easily lose one's head, so completely did the scent of roses, by who knows what deviance, besot the solar plexus and other obscure forces of devotion.

"I drink every word, my eyes fixed on her carmine lips. With the blue of the sky and the white of the walls framing her face, reality crumbles.

"Then an image straight from the land of improbability flies at me. So powerful an image that my body is hurled against hers, my mouth approaches hers, and my trembling hand seeks under her skirt and finds a new and familiar shape that changes the pace of my breathing. Then there is magic, a flawless chemistry that has me quivering with joy, and has her chanting, 'Devastate me to a dream.'

"After. I can attest that this woman's improbable ramblings entered my own life as an infinite thirst for knowledge and understanding. A veritable frenzy for reading took hold of me, but I refused to continue my studies. I devoted myself wholly to music and reading. The world was now one big performance and I very soon learned to watch it without being afraid. Yet this morning, I'll admit, that sombre voice on the radio and the stillness all around us sowed a terror in me that I can't explain.

"It's seven years now since I've been back in this country. By day I give violin lessons and by night I play at the Hotel Rafale. On Wednesdays and Thursdays I'm a soloist. On Fridays and Saturdays I'm the violinist for the Fiction Tango Quartet. I live in a neighbourhood where I have less and less opportunity to speak English. My father still lives in Buenos Aires. My mother has settled in Mendocino, north of San Francisco. I write her once a month. Making love with you stimulates me to talk."

The young woman's face had changed as she spoke of earlier days, then gradually regained its youth as she watched the expression on Cybil's face, a face that never changed on account of the three layers of happiness overlying the loneliness whenever she was concentrating.

～

Around four in the afternoon, Cybil suggested they go and walk about the city.

On leaving the hotel they turned left, the direction that leads to all delinquencies, where the heat, smells and humanity of every nobility and stupidity converge like springtime rivers chock-full of life and rubbish.

They walked a while among the tall buildings of downtown and then, lacking any landmark save the surrounding poverty, found themselves in a milieu of males adult and adolescent. Skilled street entertainers, these selfsame were exchanging dictatorial and mafioso postures in a banter of jaw and cheek, each sally more threatening than the last. Here and there a few women carried heavy bags that threw off their equilibrium. The wind whistled around them and the streets were dirty and filled with garbage. The cars drove by quickly and disappeared around a bend, leaving behind their awful afterglow, which inexorably and ominously entered people's eyes. Cybil was thinking that history is always the same, with bones watching and waiting in the midst of sensuality and pleasure. It's what is in our thoughts that renovates history. History is young and someone has packed it with dead people to make it look less empty.

Shots sounded in the distance. Cybil started. She mustn't worry about it, La Sixtine said protectively. Nothing is more civilized than walking in a city. We can't interrupt our walk because of a few suspicious sounds. The sun is benevolent. The future brings happiness if one thinks of it as a game of chance. And as if to prove that she knew violence and cruelty to be perennial, the young Sixtine alluded to an old French writer she had seen recently on television. This man had talked of the splendour and magic he had discovered as a child at the beginning of the century in the streets of Peking. He described the torture death of Leng-Tch'e. The motley crowd had pressed close while the prisoner's limbs were severed one by one and his heart was ripped from his chest. To portray the bewildered expression graven by extreme pain on the tortured man's face, the writer used the word ecstasy. He also found words to describe the distinctive smell of freshly spilled blood, and the marvellous effect made by the sun's rays penetrating the man's still-living entrails.

"I know those pictures," Cybil said. "They were first published in 1923 in a psychological treatise, then in 1961 by an author who gave them an erotic dimension." So saying, she quickened her pace and for several minutes kept muttering words whose sense escaped La Sixtine.

This aside spoken in some mysterious tongue was interrupted by the cries of a woman standing in the middle of the street waving her arms and displaying her blood-stained bosom. A policeman appeared and hastened to call an ambulance. Cybil Noland wanted to turn back but La Sixtine put her arm around her shoulders and led her down another street where the walls were covered with scrawls. A man shouted two syllables which crashed as graffiti on a wall of pink stucco. At each parking lot the city bared its aluminum teeth to the sun, and the sun multiplied the possibilities of fires and fiction. Once again, Cybil Noland felt the strength and number of those questions. She saw them swirling about her and La Sixtine like the sudden, destructive tornadoes that fill people's hearts with panic; then some of them swept away into the surrounding hovels while others ricocheted off the fronts of videoclubs which proclaimed the reign of individualism and the visual image. Slowly, the city took on tones of grey and blue.

Another street. Here and there, women with tattooed biceps and men with bare chests and pierced nipples strolled about in black boots, heads shaven. Equipped with a new vocabulary, they were leaving walls alone in favour of more direct statements in their own flesh. The men carried fear and danger in their bodies, arming themselves only for sexual encounters when the electricity of a single shot would emerge from their bodies with much noise.

Cybil's thoughts ground to a stop in a time-honoured scenario where Death weighs all with the brawny arms of an executioner. The executioner is a prince who does not count the drops of blood on his free, lonely brow. A man with much ado, he holds in his hand a chiselled jewel of culture, an uneasy member erected by who knows what misfortune, what vengeance, and kept up by who knows what hope.

⌀

La Sixtine suggested they go back to the hotel. She would have to get ready for the evening show. On the way she spoke to an old man who was playing a violin by the wall of an abandoned house. She told Cybil he was from Las Vegas where he had been a croupier for thirty years. One day, after a shooting which had brought a crowd of rubberneckers to the neighbourhood, the man had played for them, clearly pleased to have such a large audience. He played "I Did It My Way" and a sonata which moved La Sixtine. The people gradually drifted away. La Sixtine and a young Afro-American woman stuck round a bit longer. The musician stuck them with a monologue about his youth. When the black woman interrupted, demanding that he *play black*, the man heard wrong and played the first movement of the sonata over again. Then he put his violin away, speaking felicitously of the sensation that flows from the instrument through one's fingers up to the shoulder and neck before settling in one's head like a question mark over the world of the living. He used a strange comparison, saying that the hand that holds the bow must always be graceful, fertile, and excite the imagination like the gloved arms of an elegant woman. Then, with only a wave of his hand over his head for transition, he gestured to the women to leave him.

La Sixtine had invested this gesture with symbolism, associating it with a kind of noble flippancy, a libertarian use of air space. Since then she had been using it herself at the close of each evening performance. It seemed to have a magical power to ward off men with a fondness for scenarios of nocturnal adventure in which they invariably saw a leading role for the young musician.

This gesture had been the reason she had followed Cybil to her room the night before. She remembered now that after playing her final note she had forgotten to trace the fetish gesture in the smoky air. A fraction of a second then had sufficed for Cybil Noland to enter her universe. The two women had exchanged quizzical looks at the speed of blood rising to the head. La Sixtine had acquiesced with her eyes to a distant question, lured by the shadowy form of the unexpected carrying her back over the years. In the elevator, she felt both vulnerable and ready for action, a fertile cross between anticipation and tension, as excited as thirty-six lionesses advancing abreast through the savanna toward the dawn.

Back at the hotel, the lobby is full of men and women conversing. Cybil Noland goes straight up to the room while La Sixtine goes to the checkroom to retrieve her violin, her black performance dress and a makeup kit.

∾

At this time of the day the room has a dark, disquieting air. One has to turn on all the lights in order to read, write or apply makeup. La Sixtine is sitting at the dressing table, on which she has placed the makeup kit. Part of the bed is reflected in the dressing-table mirror. In the background of the reflected image, Cybil Noland lies with arms crossed behind her head. La Sixtine's face is reflected in the smaller mirror on the makeup kit. A distance separates the two women, a matter for reflection, fair game for seduction. From where she is, Cybil can see La Sixtine's image twice, her own just once at the far end of the bed where features grow hazy.

La Sixtine deftly wields her pads, pencils and brushes, makes them secrete the makeup, the powder, mascara and so on, showbiz props capable of darkening the day and brightening feelings, colours that one inserts in a dream to make the night resplendent, shining with sweet delight.

In the mirror, La Sixtine's eyes change to oblong shapes: the Udjo eye persisting in Cybil's eyes. A majestic parade of other hieroglyphs: a bird, foot, scarab, mouth, hare, like a semantic blend, an admirable and sensually genial proportioning between animal and human that occidental writing would never achieve. Then eye and words churn in Cybil's head. Sign by sign, the Hyde Park woman reappears. There she is climbing the grand staircase in the British Museum. Her red raincoat leaves a trail of light between the statues, busts and sarcophagi. She stands now before the Rosetta Stone. She's intrigued by a lion's head and wonders in what direction its meaning points.

Taken in the heat of the present day, the question stands. If life has no direction because day and night are circular, in what direction does its meaning point? Is meaning only in the question as a desire to decode lives that advance the story of the world by ramifying acts and intentions? Was meaning totally hidden in the means of survival, the tools and strategies devised for facing up? A dream-face versus the sur-face of daily life.

Imagination used to give life another twist, implying that life had meaning. When the impression was of happiness, meaning froze. When suffering showed its face, meaning made a comeback, instigated prodigious faiths and terrible altercations in the world of the living. Each altercation generated new words and forced meaning the way you twist an arm. Determination hardened. Then the *alter ego* got into the meaning act. The *alter* altered the value of signs and the *ego* began again from Go. Face-painting, tat-tooing, body-piercing, sensual overkill came one after the next. Life stumbled over values that were new. Picked itself up with horizon stuck to forehead like a screen. Generations passed one after the next. Life gave the body ammunition for life. The future swal-lowed. Death did as expected. Decode, Cybil murmurs. Decode; evaluate life's chances in view of all the signs. In each sign calculate an added value that lets one dance amid the questions and justify happiness. Square up our past mistakes so no one can get rolled.

Cybil observes La Sixtine, moved by her beauty, but soon her eyes cloud, for words and visuals enter into fearsome combat. In the eyes of mortals dying to show their humanity and win support for their dreams, will the visuals or the words win out?

Now La Sixtine is all close-up in the square makeup-kit mirror. With a brush, she carefully follows the outline of her lips, then fills them in with a bright red that glistens like a thousand scenarios in the story of women.

Cybil is on her feet. La Sixtine has closed her makeup kit. Everything becomes hazy. The moves are different from the day before. Other words, other caresses. The room fills with a very virgin energy. The bodies immolate, immobilize, are a hair's breadth from ecstasy. Eyes fall for what's invisible. In each woman's heart, time is counted by the second. In each woman, time is a precious signifier.

◇

The bar at the Hotel Rafale is filled to bursting with an enthusiastic crowd. The women are made up like La Sixtine. The men have fine moustaches like characters out of early novels. The quartet is performing wonders, smothering reality with fantasy, declaring war on care and mediocrity, bringing new light to all eyes.

Every Friday the Fiction Tango Quartet is in fine form when it strikes up *"Tanguedia III"* by Piazzola. Among the bandoneonist, the pianist, the bass player and La Sixtine, the synergy is total. Life skips about exuberantly among the sighs. With each note, it terrorizes, moves, flabbergasts, declares its love, says its goodbyes, foments inexplicable silences that slip among the listeners' legs, seizing on ankles or coiling about calves. So fiery is this life that some close their eyes to slow it down a mite.

Then it's back, here a foot, there an eye or mouth, a note melting between lips or skimming the curve of a breast.

With the lighting and the artifice of makeup, La Sixtine is singularly beautiful. Now is the hour for suppositions. Life moves on because someone somewhere, unable any more to bear the noise or silence, imagines.

La Sixtine is giving the best of herself. The best being a clever way of breaking up the normal course of things and making spirited celebration appear to be the normal course, indeed an exemplary expression of the way we are. For the moment, pleasure flows through the hand that holds the bow and from the eyes that unblinkingly absorb the strident sounds striating the melody. Cybil thinks of Luciano Fontana's paintings which, lacerated with a single stroke, open up, slash at the heart, and pose heartbreak as a fundamental question.

Sitting at the back of the room, Cybil is tasting veritable torments of pleasure. There is nothing dreamlike about her well-being. All of it is present, real, and very physical. Inordinately present. Who put this power of happiness in me? Who has made me this happy in a world of horrors? The word horror diverts Cybil's attention briefly but the present returns the stronger for it, brings her back to the raw pleasure of the sounds and heat of the bar. It's because I'm happy that I refused to give La Sixtine a story. Happiness abstracts me from the world, makes the world abstract for me.

Now the quartet is playing "Michelangelo." The audience listens with rapt attention. La Sixtine looks like the eighth wonder, standing in her black dress behind the bandoneonist.

The show ends and La Sixtine goes to the checkroom to leave her violin. The two women take the elevator. Still feeling the music, La Sixtine does not say a word. She knows nothing about the grey-haired woman she is following for a second night. Cybil Noland puts her arms around the young woman's waist.

～

In the spacious bed, La Sixtine reclines on Cybil. Face to face. The Udjo eye shines with all its power in the dim light of the room. She stays there a long time. She will be able, she thinks, to get inside Cybil's life, read what is in her soul and, caressing each wrinkle, in the lifelines on her forehead, around her mouth, under her eyes, and in the beautiful grey of her hair.

While La Sixtine muses over the mysterious graphemes drawn by time between the base of Cybil's neck and the rise of her breasts, Cybil is thinking, This woman is looking at me in the present past.

And while La Sixtine keeps trying through a thousand wiles to get inside Cybil's world of thought, an awareness of time seeps into her like a relentless ritual dance, lulling the heart with its repetition of the cycle of life and death.

Without closing her eyes, Cybil too has entered that vast space where one can move from one century to another, from one face to another, or be a child again running in the sand, or a woman reading by the sea with a fierce wind turning the pages violently and flattening her hair against her skull.

La Sixtine has slid her tongue into Cybil's ear and her fingers have wakened her belly so that the two of them might both go roaming, homing on this image and that, flying with all speed into the trap of a dream so vast one can still navigate freely inside, run oneself breathless flitting among characters with all the memory of the past and all the present one could wish for everywhere in one's mouth.

La Sixtine's moves are like stories begun, or lively, impetuous musical scores. Then life comes to the brim and overflows in every direction, and then again.

And so it will go all night. They will travel in time, leading several women's lives at once, change costumes, makeup and manners. They will hold out their arms in the darkness, casting a multitude of shadows on the walls of the room. Winged vessels, they will fly across the waves. All night long they will keep watch, will be sailor-women, the Eumenides, Amazons, madonnas and sirens. Poets in the great aquarium of the night.

RIMOUSKI

"I have always believed that literature is like the sea."

– J.-M. Le Clézio

"We are a race enslaved to narrative."

– Pascal Quignard

I

The river is an obsessive presence. An argument that sweeps away all misgivings. According to the will of the tides, it denudes the landscape, recomposes it, swallows up huge rocks by the hundreds then disgorges them glistening with Callipygian Venus rotundity among the cormorants, rails, ravens and sea lettuces.

A grey day. A vast mid-May seascape grey. An impenetrable wind, a grey mass, drives obliquely onshore toward the city, drives into Cybil Noland's eyes as she walks up Avenue de la Cathédral toward the river. Near the railway track, the Cantine de la Gare emits a strong smell of French fries which memory at once seizes upon, turning the mobile stand into a snack bar by a blue lake.

As she passes the Sens Unique bar, the cathedral and the river make an unsettling atavistic pair that stir up history, waken the old reflex of thinking about snowbound shores and the French language while the word country finds its way into a sentence that Cybil Noland is trying to finish. The cathedral's glinting spire shoots through her memory like the pain of a ghost arm.

In a week Cybil is to meet the oceanographer Occident DesRives, who has sailed all the planet's seas and oceans. A projected book about the sea. Off the Río de la Plata.

Cybil has arrived in Rimouski early so she can do some work on a curious text she wrote two months ago in Los Angeles, where she began the story. She has settled into a room at the Hôtel des Gouverneurs. Her room overlooks the river and Barnabé Island.

For over a year now, Cybil Noland has been thinking about her next novel. It was destined to take shape around something which, though still an enigma to her, would unfold majestically a few months later like a long, living metaphor, or cruelly in step with a mind that left nothing to chance. She liked this precursory state with its new dimension which made her vulnerable yet asserted itself in her as a sign of hope. A sure sign that something would come of all she had lived, thought or read, and that in the time preceding publication of this next novel she would succeed in penetrating some hitherto indecipherable secret of the human condition. For the time being there was euphoria without the narrative, a myriad of pictures each worth a thousand narratives, veiling the narrative. Each time an element of narrative was on the point of taking form Cybil would briefly let the form make its own way, then, if it became a subject, she would take note not of the subject but of how the transformation had come about.

And so the subject of her next novel might escape her for months on end, haunting and inaccessible. A subject that always seemed close yet far away, like the visual stamp of a world to be grasped, a subject buried in an appalling number of semantic permutations, lost in the vastness of space and the species, an infinitely precious world which the mind would try to reinstate in language, or imagine its unseen side.

This morning she reread several times what might be the beginning of a novel. Each time she had the same uncomfortable feeling. Without admitting it to herself, she knew she had transgressed a convention observed by those who since time immemorial have evaded reality the better to plunge impetuously into its spectacular, theatrical dimension wherein life's mysteries transform themselves into ornaments of speech.

Cybil knows that when she gave her own name to the Hotel Rafale woman she had committed an error in judgement which could compromise her, deprive her of the liberties, rages and extravagances in her writing that would allow her to meet imagination's challenge. Cybil Noland the character compromises the existence of Cybil Noland the writer. It could be that Cybil Noland is only a chance namesake, she thought, in which case I have no reason for worry. The woman was trying by a thousand wiles of intellect to make the error right and justify an audacity whose narcissism put Cybil off a bit. Because she could not yet put a name to what she had done, Cybil's discomfort persisted, dangling her over a critical void.

Between one thought and the next, Cybil remembered a conversation she had had five years earlier with Nicole Brossard, a novelist she had met in London at a conference on autobiography. They had spent a lot of time together, rendezvousing every morning for breakfast and in late afternoon at a Covent Garden pub. They talked for hours about books they had read and their writing, what it meant to them. One day the novelist had said, "You can't get at the essential by putting your own little self at the centre of the action any more than by finding fault with it, yet if one character, the real one, stays boxed up inside you, all the others will be crazed with grief. Or superfluous. Half of what you think is fiction and the other half is spread around the body like a play of light and shadow."

She spoke with much passion and conviction, leaning her elbows on the table and looking Cybil straight in the eye. The waitress had brought them each a second beer. A strong, dark beer whose flavour seemed to have word-productive properties. Brossard continued, asserting that it was absurd to expect to remain oneself on entering a fictional world, even wedded to the truth of one's most outlandish dreams.

Cybil didn't like to contradict her. She changed the subject by asking why she so often gathered her characters around a restaurant table or desk. "I probably don't know enough about suffering to know what's going on in people's hearts" was Brossard's reply, and she turned her head toward the newsstands around which milled a crowd of tourists and idlers, giving Cybil ample time to contemplate her aquiline nose. To break the silence, Cybil asked how the novelist came to have that French name. "Brossard was my mother's name. My father's name was Reed Vanguard. I might have written in French. I chose to bear my mother's name and write in Mr. Vanguard's language."

From the word mother on, Cybil's thoughts took another course and soon she was back on a beach at Lake Echo, in her childhood. Mothers and their children. Children and their noisy games. On Saturdays and Sundays, daddies standing with backs to the beach, smoking big cigars and talking boats and barbecues. The mothers have enormous breasts. There's a lot of beard on the fathers' legs. The women are sitting on low chairs. Some are kneeling in the sand, blowing a child's nose, adjusting a bathing-suit shoulder strap or energetically applying an orange suntan cream to the bodies of their progeny. Family chitchat, mothers whispering of minor misadventures, planning careers for their children, sighing over a sister-in-law's illness. A tall, tanned, black-haired woman is sitting in front of Cybil. When she crosses her legs, Cybil detects between the inside of her thigh and her bathing suit a tuft of hair that glistens in the morning sunlight. The roar of an outboard motorboat drowns out the voices. Then there's a lapping of waves and Cybil drops off to sleep on the blue whale adorning her beach towel.

She had been rereading her text for close to three hours now, drifting from one scene to another. Nothing was happening that might bring her closer to romantic convention. She took a sweater and went out for a walk in the city streets, keeping up an unavowable hope, that real life would be so uneventful that she would have no other choice but to return with all haste to her room and get back to the city armed to the teeth and puzzling over Cybil Noland.

She finds walking in the city reassuring, for she has always associated walking with the notion of freedom. Body in motion, constant stream of thoughts which, though induced by dogs barking, curses and those universal fuck-offs flying about like pinballs, still reflect our mindfulness of light and the full implication of the words that surround us. The city, though peaceful, raises a bundle of questions that lie brooding in the pervasive grey of the day. People go in and out of small shops that sell chewing gum, fishing gear and lottery tickets.

On the quieter streets, tall staircases and long porches whose banister rails look from a distance like tibias. Farther still, silence. In a way, life here relies justifiably on the beauty of the river. The wind sweeps away the urban din, softens the commercial bustle, so that passersby can easily be mistaken for figures all alone between earth and sky. Cybil begins to doubt the existence of cities armed to the teeth. A slow, insidious doubt grows as the day lengthens so that by four o'clock, after taking a chair on the Terrace Saint-Germain, the novelist is overcome by an immeasurable feeling of futility. For if the armed city does not exist, why describe it, why worry whether it exits or not, why condemn it? "Half of what you think is fiction." So compare!

Later, in the evening while Cybil is walking by the river, the certitude will come to her that one should not compare cities or human beings or a river with the sea. And yet the best way to illustrate what one has to say, to keep one's eye sharp and ready to intervene in a story, is by comparison. Comparison is our lasting solution in life.

2

The few letters she had received from Occident DesRives had left her with a good impression, one of a woman she imagined to be courteous, efficient and convivial. Her epistolary style Cybil thought enchanting. Occident DesRives had a gift for interweaving working hypotheses, the day's schedule and charming expressions pertaining to ocean currents, seafloor ooze and the chain of life, all in a single paragraph. From the very first letter she had won Cybil's attention by mentioning Jules Verne, Melville, Leonardo da Vinci and Joseph Conrad. She had also recommended *The Oxford Book of the Sea*.

After the second letter, Cybil began fantasizing about Buenos Aires and the Río de la Plata. She would picture herself walking the streets of Buenos Aires at night amid the strains of the tango. Occident DesRives was with her. They were walking arm in arm like *porteñas*.

In her third letter, Occident said again, "You'll have all the freedom you could wish. As they say here in hockey circles, I want heart, I want your passion." The sentence concluded with an exclamation mark in the shape of a dolphin.

Cybil played hard to get. She replied only by fax, scribbling two or three lines to say she was thinking about it. Each message was immediately followed by a letter from Occident. Sometimes it contained a nomenclature featuring flying fish, trigger fish, yellow-tailed doctor fish and trumpet fish, or Occident might talk about instinct and intelligence, dominance and submission, procreation, territoriality, and attraction exerted by females. In another missive, she explained core-sampling and ultrasound procedures. Another time she described the activity on the bridge during watch changes. She ended this letter with a description of a sunset at sea and it seemed to Cybil that the few words designating the sea and the ball of fire hanging over the horizon concealed an inordinate quest for the absolute.

At night in her dreams, Cybil swam in limpid waters with fish swimming by in schools, fish with scarlet cheeks, borne lovingly like jewels by the blue light of the water. One morning she woke in a sweat, frightened to have seen a female anglerfish, terrified to have been touched by the great sea-serpent that keeps describing an Arabic letter, always the same, in the murky depths.

The day after this nightmare, a letter arrived enclosing a catalogue of the most recent exhibition of works by Irène Mage. This was the first time Occident had mentioned that a photographer might figure in the project. Cybil felt a little twinge of disappointment. She had imagined the project to be strictly between her and Occident: science and letters. No pictures.

Cybil knew the woman's work. She had seen two of her exhibitions. All her pictures were in black and white. Cybil knew of only one in colour, "The Cruel Triptych," which had made her famous. On the left it showed Montreal lit up at night; in the centre, a park with a red dress laid out under a tree; on the right, a wedding ring and a knuckle-duster on a kitchen table. The work had drawn endless commentary.

While reading through the catalogue, Cybil wondered for the first time why Occident had chosen two partners whose work would not appeal in the least to fish.

Then one day Cybil wrote to Occident agreeing to meet her on her return from Los Angeles. In the month of May. She did not mention Irène Mage.

3

Today, sunshine. A light so beautiful it makes one feel that no one on this earth will die ever more. Because of the light, Cybil has determined that the time has come to resolve the name question. At worst, she will have to bury it by diverting attention to La Sixtine. Already she is imagining herself at the opera, sitting in the same row as La Sixtine and the admiral's wife. From there she can observe them. She is reassured by their presence. Soon, however, the name Cybil Noland reappears, totally obscuring the character. So there's to be no letup in the questioning. This woman will have to be made to speak. Bring myself into her world without breaking the thread, however tenuous, of the story begun in the room at the Hotel Rafale.

Knowing someone's story amounts to depriving her of her present. Light exists only in the present. Beautiful, pure present. Knowing Cybil Noland's past, even imagining it, amounts to taking away her present.

The tide has begun to ebb. The rocks are still no more than little bowler hats glistening in the radiant sunshine. Two hours from now there will be something obsessive about their number and shape, and the horizon will be a moonscape. Desolated.

Light, Cybil thinks, is a difficult subject to dwell on because as soon as the sun is up, colours take over and divide reality into a thousand words and objects among which one has to live all day long, thinking how heavily the visible world weighs in one's awareness.

It must have been noon when Cybil Noland picked up her camera and left the Hôtel des Gouverneurs. A man opened the door for her, muttering crossly, "Gotta look after our womenfolk."

First go and eat at La Nature. Later, walk toward an immense building, probably the university. Climb the steep slope up Rue Jean-Brillant. Puffing, Cybil found herself near the railway track. All it had taken was a walk of five hundred metres for the city to acquire an air of vacancy and silence, and the river was like a blade laid on the earth there beneath the sky, a blue hero at rest.

The cemetery brings the city to an end. It is filled with names graven in collective memory. Here life starts all over again with its birth dates, baptismal names and parents' names, its rich and its humble, its bouquets of flowers and angels and frightening allegories.

Time works like a rodent building its future. Double-faced, it creates twists and turns and blockages, then, without warning, mercurial as all creation, it fills one's eyes with sybaritic energy.

Hair streaming in the wind as if she's at the rail of a transoceanic liner, Cybil leans on her lingo and gazes into the distance while the north wind, the die that desire would cast, equating not pure chance but a merry-go-round of words, fans those extra-delectable thoughts that carry her across the centuries.

During these all-too-beautiful days of May, Cybil can thus plunge directly into an idle absolute and at the same time turn toward the essential sea, for when all is said and done, time that has nothing to prove is as smooth as a nice white page that has yet to know humidity.

In some places, in many places even, the earth seems cool and well turned over. In Buenos Aires there's probably no earth at all in the cemetery. Stone does the job. They wall in, plaster over, sweep up, but they don't dig, they don't turn the earth over. Among the shadows there, the light ignites fire on bronze and diverts the attention and respect that people owe the dead. When it alights with spectacular effect on the wings of an angel, or coils about a stele like a handsome snake attracted by the warmth, the light is signalling us to move along.

In a cemetery, the living should be able to carry on in place of time and thought, of the wish for life, of all that characterizes each generation's thoughts and imagery: life with its proper names, its rituals in the rain and snow and in the splendour of May, which brings a slightly absent look to people's eyes.

There are no carvings here to ennoble death. Only a succession of deaths upon which future generations are hidden away in notarial deeds.

Cybil walks about among the graves, looking for familiar names. Someone is walking along a path. Cybil approaches and, holding out her camera, asks for a photograph of herself beside the tombs. She smiles as she did last year at Père-Lachaise Cemetery in Paris beside the graves of Gertrude Stein, Édith Piaf and Marcel Proust. She feels absurd. The stranger walks away. His footsteps on the gravel path crunch in the warm air. At Père-Lachaise she had felt she was in a museum. It was easy to forget the dead, there among the tall trees, the statues and the light filtering down through the centuries. There, she smiled naturally and with pride as though she had taken Proust's arm or felt Stein's hand on her shoulder. There, her smile made sense. Here, the solitude is misleading her reflexes.

The song of a cardinal. A field mouse scurrying between the tombs. In the distance, the river. Family names. Cybil takes several pictures for later when she will want – she doesn't yet know what.

4

On the fourth morning the telephone rang and an old friend who had learned that Cybil was in Rimouski suggested they go to Sainte-Flavie for lunch. They could stop at Sainte-Luce-sur-Mer where Jasmine had a cottage. Cybil agreed. The day was perfection, like a blue-sky day in Provence. In the hotel lobby, Jasmine presented Cybil with a copy of her latest collection of poems, a token of friendship and continuity, a presage of their conversation which would surely lead them to examine together the fever of people living in perpetual fear, in times of peace and war alike.

In the car, Cybil, who had not opened her mouth for three days, talked volubly about fiction as a platitude that gives the illusion that one can either taste reality twice as well or send it packing as long as one has enough electricity between one's teeth to dare it. And eyes sharp enough to cut out scenery that's needlessly upsetting. Jasmine kept driving and lighting another cigarette. Cybil kept her eyes on the sea.

They drove for twenty minutes and stopped at the Sainte-Luce-sur-Mer cemetery. Jasmine said she wanted to be buried here, right beside the sea. Cybil took a few pictures. The sea everywhere. A few tombs. The humblest as white as chalk. The grandest with a Virgin and a Christ.

The cottage is a few feet from the sea. Low tide. Books are part of the house, like those "powerful shoulders"[3] that slow the reckless pace of progress, protect against ignorance, enfold in lucidity.

Jasmine opens a bottle of white wine. Looking out at the sea, Cybil says that this is a place made for writing. She takes two pictures. Jasmine with the sea behind. The sea by itself. In the living room, later, they talk about friendship, about death and the way it's beginning to divide reality in two, about literature which shrinks from facing up with its tormented eye but is constantly tantalized by the universe, a window or a tree for example. Paradoxical literature that fills you with enthusiasm despite repetitions and relapses, despite your thinking you could really hit the pits if you can't find the words, if there aren't words there any more to lift you back to the light of day. The way we seem. The way we are when we show up exhausted among our referents, which hurt because of speedy visuals that gobble up meaning as fast as it appears.

The sun moves across the room. The cigarette smoke scatters the light as in a theatre. Jasmine gets up, refills the wineglasses. The conversation shifts to everyday life in Rimouski. Cybil asks if Jasmine knows Occident DesRives. Jasmine discourses at length about a happy scientist. A surrealist. An intelligent and healthy-minded woman. An enigma for less fortunate folk with word-driven minds and hearts.

It's time for lunch. Jasmine puts the bottle and glasses away. Closes the shutters.

At Sainte-Flavie they came to a stop at the Capitaine Homard restaurant with its lobster-explicit sign. There they drank muscadet, ate crab and talked, one in her mother tongue, the other in another tongue with which mothers have been known to slake a thirst for knowledge. Cybil complicated things by saying that the idyllic mother-and-child image is often erased with a single headstrong stroke by men projecting their adult bodies into a realm of mirrors, the aura of the self.

Between sentences they tackled their crabs' legs, inserting a knife into the white side of the shell then drawing the meat out with a forefinger. A sip, a mouthful, then they would resume their conversation after wiping their mouths so the words would come out better, more precise, more worrisome, for the world all around had been designed so as to prevent escape from the geometry of abysses and bottomless lakes, from reflections off water surfaces and off suffering. And since both of them had so long ago taken the writer's vow, they worried over the heavy cords of suffering around the world, a world tied up like Christo's packages.

They drank a lot of coffee after their wine and talked about Venice and "the future forever put off till later."[4] Around five o'clock they set off to return to Rimouski. In the far distance, the bluffs of Bic were transforming the river into a southern sea and Cybil felt the ocean slipping into her thoughts.

La Sixtine came and sat at the end of the bed, a towel about her hips and her back glistening with dancing drops of water. Cybil Noland took her in her arms. With a series of slow, deliberate movements, she drew La Sixtine's head against her breast so that their bodies formed a huge *pietà* in the middle of the room.

5

Where do we get the idea that we absolutely have to shake up our thoughts at regular intervals in hope they'll fall into place the right way up, in word couples or families. Even if words build palaces with the gloomy side of our desires, we mustn't go throwing ourselves on them hoping for miracles.

She always works with notes and never knows what comes from her heart or head or from the story line. It's five o'clock in the morning and high tide. Like a giant submarine, Barnabé Island keeps watch between the North Shore and Rimouski. Cybil leafs through an illustrated Cousteau book. Her thoughts flit from corals to seaweeds to starfish. Two days to go before the meeting. The silence in the room spells out her name. Life's meaning rises to her throat like a necessity. We cannot ask desire to point a finger at the centre for us and at the same time demand that it regulate our rhythm, add water to the sea, memory to our bodies and excitement to what we write. Do ideas that come to us at the height of libido leave us after a time? Do they turn into peaceable pussycats generously offering all nine lives to be stroked, confident that the beauty of the day will waken a few more fantasies in us?

The sun is coming up. Words shuttle back and forth between the far reaches of an idea and its surface images. Just when you think they're there to stay or to enflame the senses, the words slip away from what we intend, drift randomly, multiply like the humpbacked rocks in the river or make eddies in the cool morning air.

Los Angeles reappears, a great deserted parking lot ringed with palms. A couple of women are crossing the street. There's no centre any more. The river licks at the Hyde Park woman's feet.

Everything is muddling. The price of books is going up. Visuals breed more visuals. The number of births doesn't match the number of love stories. In each woman are several centres. One only of gravity. People use the word sporadic often and exquisite less and less. The river destroys the idea of centre. Storytelling is not enough. Playing is a symptom of freedom. Looking at the river is enough. Anyone who writes should always bring pleasure to anyone dying to do likewise. In a way. Life offers its thousand broad backs, which are its shell. "Tracking" en route for a new world, ideas excite the life principle in those great bodies said to be of love that we invent to bring us closer to the light.

Cybil Noland collected subordinate clauses, wondering what the world would be like if it had to be conceived in short sentences. A spell of harmony in each. Or if the verb "to be" had to be used repeatedly. What if we could divide the silence in our universe into bands of equal reach? What if, on the other hand, we had to imagine reality by constructing long sentences ready at all times to change direction, to bring on strong new sensations, bungee-wise, in heads longing for headlong dives? What would reality be like if we had to spin out its features like a conversation in which we're tested by marks of affection and hostility? How does reality, so compact deep down in us, manage to unfold by generating sites of horror and at the same time visions of the future that blow our minds, like love and total void?

Reality is compact.

Fascinated by the direction her thoughts are taking, Cybil has raised a hand, ready to touch. Slowly, the silence makes its appearance. More slowly still, it makes like a character. Then it monopolizes attention, causing the furniture in the room and the Stanley Cup on the cover of the television guide and the matchbooks distributed in the ashtrays to disappear. The silence takes Cybil by the hand and walks, leading her to a place open to the sky where thousands of books lie exposed to all Nature's vicissitudes, propped one against another: rare books, early books, atlases, pocketbooks. An open city of books.

Though Cybil has raised her hand, her fingertips find nothing. Just a strong, bewildering sensation that assaults her neurons. The sensation quickens the beating of her heart and changes her rate of breathing. The sensation travels clear across the room. It takes over in the novelist's disoriented body.

Touch reality as if it were an unwound tape of the mysteries of writing. Touch ever so gently that which alters time and feeds hope, boosts the volume of cries and lamentations, golden words always ready to amplify our senses and satisfy our lioness appetites.

Touch in hope of understanding how, in a hotel room, it's easy to take oneself for a character in a book. But then the character changes. Her facial expression keeps changing because the thinking side of her puts her firmly on notice to get moving toward a better life, a fascinating subject. The name Cybil Noland floats in the air. Standing at the window, Cybil has no trouble recognizing her own shadow hanging about the river and the light.

Yes, she would have liked to get a feel of compact reality in order to strengthen her eye power and the new faculties that develop when an eye shines. For an eye that shines is always closer to perfection than life that has let itself be torn in two by night since time began.

Cybil looked out at the river. Reality was simple under the window of her room. People were parking their cars, getting out and slamming the doors. The men were putting on their sunglasses. The women were straightening their skirts. They were coming for the buffet lunch at which they could have all the clams they could eat. On Sundays they would bring the children and grandparents for brunch. Others would be going next door to the Marie-Antoinette and still others to the Saint-Hubert B.B.Q. while waiting for the bus to Rivière-du-Loup or Montreal.

Writing had widened the gulf between reality and thought. Then had patiently filled it in, partly with a chorus of worried I's launching, with heads full of questions, on the adventure of this writing "thing," which today had grown so enormous that thought would go straight to visual synthesis to sum it up.

Later that evening Cybil has crossed the big parking lot where the wind off the river always brings a shiver. A look all round before entering the Dallas Bar, where women are trying to ease reality by pressing their heads to the chests of silent men preoccupied with bad puck-passing by the Nordiques.

"That's life," says the woman, putting her handbag on the table. Cybil doesn't object. The woman goes and dances, closing her eyes. She comes back. Cybil lights a cigarette. The woman talks a lot. Nothing happens because she talks about things elsewhere, mixing in her children and the father and an uncle at the end of a wharf at twilight. She goes and dances with another woman, "My ex-sister-in-law." She comes back and Cybil lights another cigarette. The woman comes here three times a week, "nights when it's quiet an' I c'n spot guys fast that look like good clean fun," she says before ordering another beer. She cries and blows her nose on the paper napkin Cybil has just scribbled a few words on, then goes and gets another so Cybil can write her name and Montreal telephone number on it. "Jis' in case I up'n git some day fer a better life." Cybil doesn't write her name; she stands up, says she has to go home. Before leaving she casts a final eye round the room. The woman is sitting at the bar. A man is offering her a drink and a cigarette. As she leaves she hears Linda Ronstadt's voice beginning "Blue Bayou."

Outside, the wind nips at her cheeks. The night comes alive in the mother tongue. She goes back to Room 43 at the Hotel Rafale. The river is a river of ink. Cybil will write all night with her head pressed to the thoughts of Cybil Noland. Making her talk.

6

Sixtine, the silence is spinning. The sea comes vast vital to those great contented, black-painted eyes of yours that you offer as a passage in time. The softness of your skin prepares my words so I'll know from which of many vantage points in memory I speak. Something fluid and tempestuous stirs the thought in me that one can create voices and at the same time isolate one's own so as to lose none of the meaning that rises from the planet.

With that scarlet mouth pressed to my temple, perhaps you might capture some of my thoughts, snatching them from the tumult of their flight.

I belong to an era when books were objects of desire and knowledge. Yes, back then they caused people to tremble with excitement, fear and pleasure. Sometimes they created a stir that lasted for weeks on end. Through books, life could draw enrichment from taking liberties with thought. They could give meaning to life because it was in them that meaning was developed, and fifty or a hundred years later ideas might struggle to life or slowly die. Both tradition and change came from books. The dream thread running through them brought such light to reality that for the subtlest of scenarios reality seemed assured. Good and evil used to rub shoulders in books and engage in fierce combat which implanted the germ of certainty that injustice and untruth must be fought against. On occasion books would also arouse such jollity and pleasure that for a few days one would willingly allow oneself to wallow in iniquity and sacrilege. Perversions, passions and unmentionable things slipped between their pages. In them could be found landscapes visible only to reading eyes. Sixtine, those eyes could trace, in the blinding whiteness of noon in July, the path of a breeze blowing from the summit of desire to the naked shoulder of a woman asleep on the grass; those eyes allowed one to hear, yes, hear the cooing of the free *paloma*. Those eyes could even detect the tiny gleam that appears sometimes in the eyes of poets just before they're seized with the fever and t/error of writing. As for smells and flavours, cries and lamentations, kisses and caresses, only the eyes of the heart could amplify their feeling.

Back then, the smell of books could be intoxicating. It took the smallest spark of memory to make one's heart race and come within a hair of ecstasy. Exciting, dangerous, that's what books were. So they had to be chosen meticulously and handled lovingly. A good number were forbidden because they might enflame whole populations, make them run about and sing, or launch them headlong toward the future. Now that the present-future of the planet is turning to potluck full-speed-ahead, books, except for sacred books which have always endangered women's lives, at most serve only for reflecting on a few open wounds.

I learned to seek the company of books when I was very young. I knew all the libraries and bookstores in my neighbourhood. Wherever there was a book – in a restaurant on the table between two cups of tea, in a garden on the knees of a woman with gaze chock-full of meaning, in a stroller wedged behind the backrest and the child, lying in the sun on the back seat of a car, tucked under the arm of a passerby or protruding from a handbag – I could spot it.

In public places, I was fascinated by the capacity for concentration of anyone turning a page in the midst of noise and movement. On the readers' faces I watched the passage of fearsome battles, bitter scenes of jealousy, and the ensuing anguish and sorrow. Often the women would sigh as they read, holding their books at arm's length, astonished that so much madness and excess could find place in the language and do it honour. The men, in contrast, drawn by the reflection of souls they took to be their own, would bring their books respectfully toward their eager faces.

I still talk about certain characters from books because these creatures of fictional flesh, having passed through our lives, often play a major role in a phrase or visual impression or feeling of déjà vu. Or is it perhaps that we ourselves, reaching out with our thoughts like great magic arms, manage to demonstrate a richly fertile imagination?

I can see myself at seven years old, walking beside a tall sailor. He had come to live at our house. He was a distant relative of my mother's. He was handsome, I think, though it's vague in my memory. All I remember is his lower jaw and his white uniform. He must have been twenty-something.

In the months he lived with us, it was his duty to take me to the movies on Sundays while my parents were having an afternoon rest. His name was César. On the way to and from the movie house he would talk to me as if I were an adult, which made me think that I was perhaps his only confidante. There were days when he told me, "I have a breastplate instead of a heart." On other days he would declare, "I don't have a heart any more. No one can hurt me there. I'm invulnerable." Then he would tell me about the ships arriving in distant ports. He would describe the swarming mass of the motley crowd, the colours of the fabrics, the smell of saffron and cumin, and the suffocating heat. He never talked about the sea, except for what drove up the price of love while in port. He talked about unsavory, dangerous bars frequented by hookers and by musclemen who fought together with long knives and such terrible utterances that peace seemed improbable forever after.

We used to stop often on the way, he to bend an elbow, I for an ice cream. At the movie he would snore while my little girl's eyes were open wide to Greta Garbo's beautiful face. With all my being I would struggle to hold her back, keep her from throwing herself under the terrifying wheels of that train from hell, that murderous machine thundering down on us.

I still wonder how a child of seven could soak up all that man's babble. It was probably because of books. I had been reading adventure novels for a year. Through them I had become an adventurer, an explorer. I knew those immoral, unwholesome ports César talked about because I had already been there. It was just his talk about the breastplate that puzzled me. I couldn't make up my mind whether he wore a breastplate under his uniform, had had an operation on his heart, or had invented all that to make himself interesting. One thing is certain – by our third outing, I wanted a breastplate too. Then I would be able to come to the rescue of girls in my class whom young pirates with sharks' eyes would terrorize at the least opportunity.

After César left, I begged my mother to buy me a centurion's breastplate and a book I had seen in a bookstore window and become truly obsessed with. The name of the book was *Les misérables*. On the cover, a little girl of seemingly immeasurable sadness was imploring me to come to her aid. I had to have the book so I could know the little girl, and the breastplate so I could protect her and bring back her smile.

Though my mother refused to buy me the breastplate, she did get me the book.

This is how a taste for travel and combat and a love of women and books have come together in me as a living whole. The things we want from life enter us in a curious way, and change just as mysteriously with the thirst for knowledge that's at work in us like an instinct.

Our happiness decides. Our life is a living dream translating its course.

7

It's nine o'clock when Occident DesRives arrives at the hotel. Her face drawn from a night of writing, Cybil is waiting in the lobby, the morning's *Le Soleil* in her hand. The woman is ageless. A pink scar runs from her temple down to her chin. Her eyes, blue like the sea and the night, look Cybil over. She's wearing a blue split skirt, a leather vest, a black blouse against which hangs a narrow tie, an ambiguous ophidian shape against her chest. She casts a sweeping look about the room. Cybil advances toward her.

The oceanographer holds out her hand, her manner smiling and direct. In a few sentences she conveys the schedule for the day, which promises to be sunny, and says they'll need fifteen minutes to get to the Institut Maurice Lamontagne. Irène Mage will meet them around ten-thirty in the cafeteria. Cybil asks if they can stop in La Grande Place long enough to drop off a roll of film.

In the car, Occident talks with a lot of numerals: wave height, river width, water depth, wind velocity, numbers of employees, offices, laboratories, ships and aircraft, years spent in Rimouski, total annual grants to the Institute.

She talks fast and drives slowly. Cybil nods, envisions questions which she has no time to formulate. Occident's voice sweeps up everything in its path that Cybil hesitates to ask about. The pace with which Occident imparts her contemporary knowledge contrasts with the naturally age-old landscape. Her knowledge, the expressiveness of her face "from her chin to the roots of her hair"[5] and the light over the river in the background together form a unit of sight and sound so dense that in the closed space of the Renault 5 Cybil has a feeling of double present, a mixture of tenses that dangerously engulfs the senses. As if Occident's presence, though physically comforting, is awakening an evil portent. There is undoubtedly something fraudulent about an intelligence that keeps pointing us to the tragic art of checking off the right answers in the wrong places.

As Occident parks the Renault she says they have time to drop by her office. Key ring, lucky charm; Cybil observes the golden die among the keys.

When they enter the office Cybil is staggered by what she sees. The whole room, ceiling included, is turquoise blue. Brazen, beautiful, unsettling. Only the window wall is painted a white that frames the daylight, a precious jewel at the horizon. In the middle of the room are two desks placed face to face. On one, a computer and a printer; on the other, a notebook and pen cunningly arranged as though to please or intrigue.

A young man sits at the computer. With his hair and beard and the wiry hairs protruding from his shirt collar, he makes a dark mass against the turquoise. He stands up, taking his jacket from the back of the chair, gives Cybil a courteous nod and then speaks to Occident to tell her that he has succeeded in installing the new software program on the so-called dead seas. He leaves discreetly. As soon as he is out of the room Occident declares him to be one of the most brilliant graduate students she has ever known. "He only has two years left. Sit down. I'll be back in a second."

Cybil stays standing as she would in an art gallery. Each wall bears a poster. Cybil starts. Over there is an enormous female anglerfish identical to the one that had brushed her in one of her aquatic dreams. The fat oval shape against the black background has a huge open mouth showing two rows of frighteningly transparent teeth. Its tiny eyes, together with the dorsal fin between them that serves as antenna and lure, make it a perfect monster. On the opposite wall is a land-scape: pointed blood-red rocks thrusting into a steely grey sky in which hangs a round, sinister moon. The rocks rise out of and are reflected in water that can only be imagined to be deep and unpitying. Below the photograph is an inscription:

Sunset Over a Fractal Island. Produced entirely by computer-generated image synthesis. Relief Algorithm by B. Mandelbrot. Production by F.K. Musgrave.

The third poster is a reproduction of "The Cruel Triptych."

In the corridor, someone coughs. Occident reappears in the doorway. Cybil is sitting at the desk with the notebook. Musing, she toys mechanically with the pen. Occident stands near the "Sunset," the red reflecting momentarily on her scar. She excuses herself for her absence and goes and takes two books from the bookcase, which she asks Cybil to sign for her. "May I?" Cybil asks, indicating the pen on the desk. "That one's out of ink, take this one," Occident says, holding out a Bic. She remains standing behind Cybil. A man's perfume. "Eternity," perhaps. Her presence makes Cybil uncomfortable. Cybil gets up, takes several steps toward the window and looks out at the sea for a moment before writing eight or nine words in each of the books.

In the cafeteria, Occident heads straight for a fiftyish-looking woman who is about to put a polystyrene cup to her lips. Frowning, the woman looks up questioningly at the two women who seem to have appeared out of the blue. Although Cybil has often seen pictures of Irène Mage, she does not immediately recognize the photographer. The latter smiles in Occident's direction first and then, looking Cybil straight in the eye, pronounces a few words which Cybil takes to be friendly.

Irène Mage lights a cigarette. She seems impatient to hear Occident talk about the project. Her first question concerns the motives that led the oceanographer to pick two collaborators whose work would not appeal in the least to fish.

Occident replies that artists exist to catch people off guard and to give pleasure. Incite emotions that science cannot explain. Whatever one thinks about this, science is at the mercy of blocks of fiction it encounters as it goes along, you know, those curious masses that obstruct the passage of thoughts. Only artists have the power to turn them transparent or make them less resistant. Yes, that's it, artists can change blocks of fiction into currents of thought. But why don't we discuss that over lunch? For now let me outline the project. We'll take the plane to Buenos Aires and stay there a few days before going on to La Plata where there's an important oceanographic centre. From there we'll board the *Symbol* for two weeks, during which the team is going to be taking core samples. There'll be three divers on the mission. In their company you'll become the omnipresent eye; the only secrets the sea will have will be those you choose to let it have. Cybil, I don't know how we invent reality, or how it slips through our fingers, but I'd like everything you find pleasing, and also dangerous, repugnant, insignificant or overwhelming to become viable, authentic and magnificent through your writings.

"In all and overall, I'm asking you for three weeks of your lives. Sometimes in difficult conditions. We're going to be three women in a world of men. In close quarters. You'll have to learn to protect yourselves from the sun and wind. The boat's well equipped, there's a library that we also use as a screening room. Irène, I know you speak Spanish. Cybil, I hope the language won't be an obstacle for you. I don't know how to thank you both for coming. I really have my heart set on this project."

Occident is visibly moved and her voice suddenly seems far off, like the barely audible whisper of a kite above the glasses and packages of sugar and little cream pots scattered about the table. The double-present sensation begins again, this time accompanied by an orange sky and the recurring picture of the deep and unpitying water in "Sunset." At the next table, a woman is talking about her dream of the night before. She was giving birth to triplets during an undersea dive. Who is that speaking? A red-haired woman laughs, exclaiming, "Dreams are crazy!" Her companion, dressed in a lab coat, shakes his head as he sucks on his pipe. His feet shuffle nervously under the table. The woman laughs again. Harder, with A's that bounce in her throat until an oof pronounced off curls up like a sigh between her lips. She wipes her eyes, reaching under her glasses with two fingers, lifting them briefly to her forehead, which makes her look like an old-time aviator. The man reiterates, "Yes, crazy," and the woman laughs again, uncontrollably, shaking all over. Beyond her, Cybil sees the graduate student engrossed in reading *Le Soleil*. The lobe of his ear glints in the dark mass of his hair. A small hoop. *Puce à l'oreille* as in Rabelais's time when men took up the habit, like women, of wearing a single earring.

Occident's voice regains command over the ambient noise in the cafeteria. Irène Mage lights a cigarette. Her mouth disappears behind a smokescreen. Her eyes sparkle. Occident laughs loudly and runs her long hands through her hair. Cybil has the feeling she has missed some important moment. Occident suggests they visit the Institute before lunch.

∿

When they leave the restaurant the three women linger in the parking lot. Occident takes leave of her guests with a reminder that they are to visit the *Symbol* at ten the next morning. Irène drives Cybil back to the hotel.

The two women are silent on the way. A pleasant fatigue has filtered through their limbs and thoughts like a soothing alcoholic drink after a day's skiing. The river is once more the focus, commands total attention, provokes by dazzling with the sun's reflection.

At the beginning of the meal, Occident had carried the conversation, talking at length about the reproduction and whimsical sexual behaviour of the aquatic fauna. Mating dances and fertilization amid spines and tentacles. Under the cover of seduction there are ancestral hatreds played out. Each species has its methods of approach and dissuasion; spiny cheeks, toxic mucosae, paralyzing poisons in no way preclude rosy and fruitful romances.

From mating dances and rituals to crooning, crimes of passion and amorous parasites, the talk was all about the flesh. From there somehow the three women came around to sexual slavery, the trade in organs and grandmothers bearing their grandchildren. Soon each seemed down in the mouth. Occident maintained that science must follow its own course. In reply to Cybil's moralizing, Irène let out a great "Oh come, now!" Which moment Occident used to signal the waiter to bring some wine. Thus aided, an enthusiastic trialogue ensued, with scatterings of ideology and stinging retorts soon evolving into such scabrous remarks that one would have thought a wind of madness had seized the three women, who by now laughed till they cried.

In the car, Cybil says suddenly, "I have the impression we see sexuality the way the hermit crab and the emperor angelfish do, that is, each of our eyes sees a different thing. With one eye we make out the object of our desire, while with the other we can't distinguish between what our desire imagines and what our hormones intend."

"I see you did some research before meeting Occident."

"I read a few articles. Occident is a disconcerting woman. At times in her company I have strange sensations, as if reality were split in two."

"Lack of focus," Irene says, lightly brushing the hand that Cybil has lying near the gear shift.

"Since I began this new novel I've been dreaming a lot. I easily lose patience and the thread of my thoughts."

Irène laughs.

"That's life, you mustn't take it too seriously. Funny things happen to me too when I'm *producing*."

"That's what you call creation?"

"Of course. Why would it be otherwise? I produce flashes, short moments during which valuable slices of reality come to light. I calculate. I flash. I rush. I feed the curiosity of the eye. I find a title. Emotion follows or it doesn't. I don't want to offend you, Cybil, but it seems to me you're pretty naïve about what you call creation. And don't answer that by telling me I'm cynical."

The car stops at a traffic light. Irène turns to Cybil and looks at her thoughtfully.

"You work in depth. You get inside your subject. That's what every writer hopes to do, surely: get to the bottom of human nature by digging in the dictionary, in history and in one's own slimy little memory which brings back one's earliest primal feelings. The best you can hope for is to touch bottom. The more you excel in your art, the deeper you get in the dark world of passions and motivations. Your art execrates superficiality and speed. It remains profoundly moral. Where you dig down, I look for surface plays, appearances, illusions. The more I perfect my art, the more I master light. We are eyes first and foremost, Cybil, and these eyes are made for undoing the reality of the world."

The car has come to a stop in the parking lot of the Hôtel des Gouverneurs, where Irène booked a room this morning before continuing on to the Institute. She suggests she meet Cybil in the bar in an hour. Her tone is as light as if she has just finished talking about the weather.

Cybil walks toward La Grande Place where she will pick up the prints of the film she dropped off this morning. The wind, always the wind while crossing the parking lot. Sounds of car doors slamming and engines starting. High heels ringing on the tarmac. Escalator. Lingerie shop. Candy shop. Stationer's. Pharmacy. Record shop. Tobacconist's. Coupon, change, thank you. Smiles. Pictures. Twelve pictures which Cybil looks at without delay. Four taken from the hotel room. The inescapable parking lot, two lamp standards, gaunt grey trees, a one-way street with its red rectangle; then three of the river, flat and grey and out of proportion with reality. Rue de la Cathédrale: a parking meter, a Canadian flag, a Quebec flag, parked cars. The river in the background. The three backlit pictures of the cemetery show no more than fragmented shapes. The picture of Jasmine and the one of the sea at Sainte-Luce are perfect. The two remaining are from last Christmas. They are almost identical except that in one of them Cassandre Noland's eyes are closed, probably blinded by the camera flash. Her mouth is laughing amid hollow cheeks and wrinkles. A decorated tree behind her. Small red and green bulbs glow beside her white hair. Her right hand rests on the arm of the chair, the other lies still on a knee. Cybil's eyes cloud. She puts the pictures back in the envelope. In the parking lot a car almost hits her. She gives the driver the finger. He brakes and backs up, threateningly. Cybil hops over a parapet. The car takes off again. *"Ma tabarsnake!"* is snatched away by the wind.

In her room, Cybil makes a note of Irène's scandalous remarks, underlines "touch bottom," makes a phone call to Montreal. There's no reply at her sister's where Cassandre Noland lives. The pictures lie spread out on the bedspread. Mother, I love you so! You who no one ever took seriously. You who predicted unerringly what each of your children would become, but who never found words to imagine what I am.

Mother, to say your name, Mother, to say I think of you busily orchestrating each day in its smallest details. I can hear every one of your interdictions, delivered with dignity. Yes, Mother, you were a joyless woman. Mother manifest who knew the fragility of things, since the world out there displayed its hopelessness. Little Mother, a mighty presence in the living room where you were always reading, your eyes turned to the thousand dangers lurking in the gloom of your imagination.

Cybil's mind wanders briefly amid a strange syntax in which visuals spit forth ugly sounds. The telephone rings. Irène Mage is at the end of the line, sounding in a hoopla mood. She is insisting that Cybil meet her in the bar. The photographer is in fine form, or fine chaos form, ready for a long evening, it seems.

When Cybil enters the bar, there is such a mixture of impatience, weariness, and intelligence in her eyes that Irène thinks it well to keep her distance. Cybil cannot decide whether this reserve is dreaminess, seductive strategy or a return to good manners. She sits down and glances at the television screen where hockey players are boarding each other roughly along very noisy boards.

Ready to join in conversation the way others join battle, Noland turns to Mage. For the first time, she feels she is actually seeing the woman. Her short hair, bluish grey. Her eyes too, but of another grey, of rare transparency. The same grey that had intrigued Montreal critics and caused much ink to flow at the time of her first exhibition. Her wrinkles are all concentrated around her eyes and mouth. Her forehead and cheeks are as pale and smooth as Italian marble.

Irène lights a cigarette. Sounds of skates scraping on the ice, the puck thudding against the boards, the shouts of the crowd punctuate the hum of muffled voices in the bar.

Noland would like to return to what Mage was talking about in the car. Mage looks around her with wild-animal eyes. Finally she speaks.

"I've only read one of your novels. The story takes place in London. The passage that moved me most was the visit to the British Museum where your heroine meets a novelist. The two women are looking at a photograph. The novelist strikes up a conversation. They never look at each other. They stand side by side. The heroine is wearing a red coat. You don't say anything about their faces. About their expressions. You observe what they do. A leg that moves, a hand on a hip, a step forward. The novelist runs a hand through her hair. The narrator's presence, yours, behind her is obsessive. Once in a while when one of the women moves slightly you can see a piece of the photograph. You can't make out the subject of the work."

It's years since Cybil published this book. She vaguely remembers the passage, which could not have taken up more than seven lines in the novel.

"Well, you see," Noland says, "that's exactly why literature has meaning. Because of these details finding their way into the mind, becoming encrusted in one's memory like tiny crystals of life. You never know when they'll resurface or bring together other things we carry around in us like an affliction, a latent feverishness."

"Forgive me for this afternoon. I don't know what got into me," Mage says, pressing the palm of a hand to each eye. "I really don't know what to think any more. That's why I accepted DesRives's offer. I've been working with computer-ized pictures for two years now. That's two years since I last set foot in my darkroom.

"It all began with my mother's death. I felt infinite tender-ness for her. When she died, an image in me shattered. In this period I began to keep company with a friend, a computer graphics designer, who was also feeling desperately low because his lover had died. At first our meetings were filled with confidences and mutual compassion. Each of us would weep in front of the other without the least embarrassment. Not just once but a hundred times we told each other about our childhoods, our loves, our adventures. He would make coffee. We would smoke. He would take out photograph albums and slowly turn the pages, pointing to the young man who appeared in every picture. After a while he would let his finger rest on a eucalyptus tree, a rock, an opossum. Then he would praise the calming effect of the Australian desert where he had met his adored Adonis. For my part, I had only to say a few words about my neighbourhood when I was a child and I would see my mother running with open arms to meet her little schoolgirl with the frosty-cold winter cheeks. She would kiss me on the nose, then go back to her kitchen and whip up a big dish of something or, well, some zen thoughts.

"Two months went by this way, with visits together every day. Then my friend began to talk about his work and research. With time, the talk turned into long monologues which I found harder and harder to interrupt with a question, observation or opinion. Every time I opened my mouth, his words would very soon engulf mine the way quicksand swallows stones and what-ever else is thrown there, and anyone who ventures into it. I'd come away from these meetings all worked up, totally incapable of understanding what he was really saying yet held breathless by the roiling of ideas and expressions.

"He could talk for hours without tiring and without touching base with reality. Rare were comparisons in his nevertheless impassioned mouth. His words would describe great zigzags about the living room, seeming to butt against invisible obstacles and each time correcting their course, making strange loops, graceful Laminaria suspended in mid-motion by time until other sentences would burst into flower, their rhythms ruled by the words law, chance and chaos, disconcerting me.

"He would move between the piano and his desk, past the computer, sit briefly at the piano, then go toward a big window through which flaming October was entering the room. A tall cheval mirror reflected October back to me with the high tree-tops on Rue des Érables beyond, while the loquacious man's body began its pentagonal path all over again. When he reached the window he would pause for a fraction of a dust-speck of silence, from which I hoped each time to launch some words of my own. Too late, for the windbag would seize the dust-speck-second and in a wink make it fractal."

Cybil gives a start.

Irène glances at the television screen. They're showing a replay of a goal scored by the Nordiques. From this point on, the bar becomes so lively that the two women retreat to Irène's room, where perhaps they'll order up something to eat and drink.

∽

The room is like Cybil's but bigger and with a living room. The curtains are not drawn. On the bed are two books, one of ocean pictures, whose cover is a blue fit to set one's eyes shimmering with delight, the other the novel *Molloy* by Beckett. "After reading your novel, I wanted to know this one. You remember – 'I am in my mother's room.'"

Sitting on the bed, the two women leaf through the picture book. Their voices blend.

"I've been having strange dreams ever since Occident first wrote me about her project. The scenes from the deepest ocean bottoms are terrifying. When I'm looking through a book from which leeches, maggots, gelatinous shapes and slimy mouths jump out at me without warning, I often have to slam it shut. I can't get used to that animal life. It's the horizontal sea, the one that's a vast surface, blue, turquoise or even grey, that excites thoughts in me. Do you expect much from this adventure Occident wants to take us on? I love the sea, but it's the one we dream about, inspires us to go voyaging, feeds the footloose in us that I love.

"I exist only with my eyes, and with the words my eyes crave when all's said and done. At the limit of my range of vision, I part with reality. Too much of life is frightening. Beside the sea I'm superbly immeasurable. Some say we feel this because of a joie de vivre that keeps validating itself by holding our eyelids open, oh, just enough so we can think we're eternal.

"The earth is too small now that we know where time goes, and how pain evaporates between the planets. That's another reason for wanting to be by the sea. The sea is our last chance for silence. Watching the clouds is a sign of humanity. Most of humanity keeps looking at the same place from the same place. Life makes you want to look the way fish do, in two directions at once. Do you think ideas can live to a ripe old age in us? Ideas are useful intuitions which, once their job is done, turn and straggle back inside what people call human nature.

"I wonder what must have been going on in the head of the first woman to finally think of the earth as round. Whether it terrified her or whether wanting to leave for distant climes, to revel in this new roundness, brought a wave of pleasure to her sex. So where is knowledge going for women? Are they cultivating it with passion or arrogance, or as something tender to be shared, something they put under their children's pillows when no one's looking so it will blend naturally with their dreams?"

∿

Now everywhere the night lies flat on the river. The room is smoky, the spaces between the sentences are longer and longer. Irène turns toward Cybil. Their eyes deliver their metaphors. The light from a lightbulb behind Irène's shoulder turns the violent inky blackness of the night to an enigmatic glow. Night brings its face close to the bay window as if to lick at the inside of the room. The two women stand side by side at the window. *Tactile,* Cybil thinks, bring out *tact, tacit, cat, act* hiding in the word. Irène places the palm of her hand where the reflection of Cybil's face in the window speaks loneliness. But there's a loving eye in Irène's hand. An eye accustomed to seeing everything. On the cold glass surface, the hand strokes the reflected outline of Cybil's face. Rediscovers the lines of her first childhood drawings, caresses the sleek black cat that used to visit the garden and stretch out under the apple tree, draws delicate circles in the fur of Maman's coat, spreads a little balm on the child's back and shoulders. Curtain.

BUENOS AIRES

"Prose is a dream falling back into reality."

– NICOLE BROSSARD

I

Leave. Conquest in mind. To write. A task for the eyes.
Take life by surprise day after day. Buenos Aires. From Room
309 at the Hotel Alvear, you watch people converging on La
Recoleta. Fatigue works to warp feelings and faces, slow-
moving questions and forthcoming landscapes.

In the plane you talked part of the night through. The atmosphere was riddled with exclamations, comments and narrative
fragments sporting convivial colours. Occident sat between you
and Irène. Whenever you turned to her, the scar imprinted its
sewn-lips pink on your sight. Irène took to beginning her sentences with "Occidentally," at which the oceanographer gave a
start each time. Irène fell asleep after the second film. You
became absorbed in a book by Silvina Ocampo. Occident
stayed awake into the early hours, arms crossed over her chest,
waiting, one would say, for the "rosy-fingered Dawn."[6]

The plane put down at Montevideo because of fog. An
hour and a half twiddling thumbs in the waiting room. On a
poster, a big seaside hotel, the Carrasco. A racking cough

shakes Occident. She takes an inhalator from her pocket. Her boarding card falls to the floor. Irène frames her bending at the waist, an arm reaching down toward the tiles. "Touching bottom." An abysmal world. Total night.

The hotel room is large and splendidly antique. The telephone rings. Occident is proposing lunch in La Recoleta. *Hasta Pronto.*

2

A year had passed between visiting the *Symbol* in Rimouski and leaving for Buenos Aires. Irène had offered to drive Cybil back to Montreal but Cybil chose to make the trip in the neutral space of the bus where, without Irène's distracting presence, she was free to feast her eyes on the beauty of the river, drink all she could of its light-drenched shores, let history bubble up in her, seeing again the big house she had been told was Victor-Lévy Beaulieu's, perched at the edge of the cliff with its fleur-de-lis flag clacking in the wind like Gaston Miron's voice, or Tolstoy's.

Back in Montreal, Cybil had resumed her daily round. The idea for a novel was evolving into a novel. The summer had been particularly sunny and so she had spent the days reading and writing in the garden. With such fulfilment for the senses, joy came frequently. La Sixtine was occupying more and more space in the novel. Her presence relegated Cybil Noland to the background, without however solving the riddle of the name. In the course of her readings and research on characterization, Cybil had discovered that John Irving, Ernesto Sábato, Wittig, Audrey Thomas, Philip Roth and Timothy Findley were also names of characters. Knowing that the taboo had been broken by not one but several others was not very reassuring, for the urge to do so could not therefore be just an author's whim. So why this contemporary urge to get inside of fiction, show off and be part of the action? Must one pledge oneself as security in case things go wrong in the narrative? An unaccustomed presence in an author's text, like the man Cybil had seen in the woods one day, holding a telephone and carrying on a conversation as naturally as you please. Was this a new way of driving fiction back to the bounds of "probably true"? Why insert one's name where the character is going to age in any event? As the months passed, the "taboo" had evolved into an archipelago of feelings where "this is my name" had shown itself to be a dazzling pyrotechnic capable of serving as signature in the contemporary sky.

On days when Cybil Noland's presence became too obtrusive, Cybil went for a walk in the Old Port. Sometimes she would board one of the ferries that plied back and forth between Montreal and Longueuil. Sitting among the cyclists and tourists, she was surprised how much those muscular calves, stalwart thighs, knobbly knees, blowing hair or streams of sweat down necks could help raise a wind of semantic tension in her.

At what moment in the eyes of the observer does a man become a cyclist, or a woman a tourist? At what point in the chain of thought can a man be said to be a pig, or a woman a cow? What clues feed an imagination which in a fraction of a second can make a man an animal, a woman a daisy, a cyclist an Italian? Would there be no letup to the injection of new configurations for the world, keeping it in perpetual unfinished recomposition yet poised to leap into the future? How can the fertile eccentricities of thought lead to the worst misunderstandings, the most idiotic misreadings of character? And depending how straight these misunderstandings go to the heart, they invest the other with imaginary power which, depending how keenly they awaken the deepest anxieties and most visceral fears, can quietly lead to war.

And so, as Cybil sought to clear her thoughts in proximity to the river and sunbathed shores, she often became lost in conjecture about what it is that so frequently leads us to relegate others to belongings of our own invention.

Curiously, the return trip to Montreal dissipated all her angst. The sight of the trees in their leafy fullness, the east-end factories, the great harbourside warehouses, the silhouette of the Jacques Cartier Bridge and the huge wheel at La Ronde reached her eyes with such luminosity that only this moment counted.

3

In the fall, during Photography Month, Cybil went to the opening of a collective exhibition in which Irène was participating. In the Dazibao Gallery's big exhibition hall, Irène was moving graciously among her friends. The woman was very different from the one Cybil had known in Rimouski. She spoke with a faintly Parisian accent and, with a confidence that one would think inbred, was dispensing intelligent and sensitive commentary to admirers capable themselves of talking knowledgeably about photography and visual representation. Irène's picture had undoubtedly been taken at the Hôtel des Gouverneurs and then reworked by computer. There was no mistaking the peaceable rounded shapes that made the horizon line.

Irène had excused herself from the group she was conversing with and came to greet Cybil. Grey of eyes and hair. Red earrings, crimson scarf, vermilion belt, like a heart exploding in three movements. The two women exchanged a few words. Cybil learned that Occident had spent the whole month of

August in Montreal. Stoically, she allowed none of her astonishment to show and asked simply if the photograph *dated*
from the Rimouski trip. Irène quickly took up the subject
with talk about pixels and silver images.

In midwinter, Cybil had gone to England and Scotland to
give three talks. At Cambridge she had renewed her acquain-
tance with Lay, a philosophy fellow at Trinity College whom
she had met three years earlier. The daughter of a wealthy
shipowner, Lay was the most eccentric woman Cybil had ever
known. The clothes she wore, her outlandish gestures, the
things she talked about and her tall stature all helped to set
her apart from ordinary mortals. In a single sentence she
might well recite a passage from *The Odyssey,* quote perti-
nently from *The World as Will and Idea,*[7] describe Charing
Cross at the height of rush hour, and spice her emotions with
a few expressions of which it would be hard to say whether
they were off-colour, in questionable taste, or just plain
vulgar. But most of all, one never knew when she was going to
dissolve into tears. The crying fit never lasted long, a mere
minute of eternity wedged between life and philosophy, then
Lay would regain her composure, brandishing her brawny
arms, which she cheerfully compared to Russian working-
women's arms. Under her left eye glistened a tiny scar, an
eternal tear. Lay's tallness had often led to misunderstanding
between the two friends. When they were both sitting, Cybil
took pleasure in everything Lay had to say, but when they
were both on their feet, Cybil had constantly to tilt her head
to look up. The muscles in her neck grew tired as when one
hunts for a book on the top shelf in a library. So when the two
were vertically positioned, Cybil, to avoid having to keep
tilting her head to put a question or make a comment, would

just nod lazily instead, staring beyond the woman's broad shoulders at small fragments of reality whose shapes stirred Bohemian hankerings in her.

After Cybil's talk, Lay had taken her to a café in Kettle Yard, then suggested they go and see Wittgenstein's grave. They had walked through some narrow city streets, along the fringe of Midsummer Common, across a bridge, then uphill along a dark street at the end of which some twenty tombstones were watching and waiting in a little wood rendered unfit for joyousness by the paucity of daylight.

After searching briefly, Lay approached a stone slab which was covered with moss and pine needles. Lud Wit stein 1889-19 . She bent over it and scratched at the dark stone with her long hands; the Austrian name and the philosopher's date of death appeared. The women stood in silence, like a pair of harps forgotten at the back of an antique shop. The cemetery was full of long roots so powerful that some of them had lifted heavy stones with grey, lugubrious corners. Here and there, everlastings brought some colour to autumn's yellow and faded green that were reminders of life's cycle. Cybil picked a wild pansy and awkwardly laid it on the grave. "Let it be said in passing: objects have no colour."[8]

In the evening, Lay accompanied Cybil to the station. The two women were standing in line at the ticket booth when Lay suddenly cried, "I'm going to London with you. We'll stay at the Dorchester. We'll drink champagne." Cybil protested that she had already booked a room for the night and absolutely had to work on the talk she was going to give in Edinburgh. Which Lay had immediately translated: *"You need material for your novel, don't you? We'll talk, eat and drink, walk silently along the Serpentine, and I shall reach out in you for the material waiting to burst out."* Cybil smiled. Lay was already stepping into a telephone booth to reserve a suite with a view of Hyde Park.

On the day she returned to Montreal, Cybil learned that a bomb had exploded within metres of the Victorian hotel. She immediately phoned Cambridge. Lay said, *"Don't worry. We all die the dark side in us shattered by love. Or a sentence, darling. Take care."*

4

On her return from Europe, Cybil had enrolled in a Spanish course at the YMCA on Metcalfe Street. Every Wednesday afternoon, after inhaling the smell of a still-brisk Montreal, she would betake herself to a wan, cream-coloured classroom where she would join ten other students, conscientiously repeating *la ventana, la silla, la lux, el lápiz, el corazón.* The instructor, Salvadorean by birth, sometimes spoke of the country she had left in tragic circumstances. When the word monkey occurred, she recounted an anecdote which stood in strong contrast with the fat, easy life of Montrealers. During coffee breaks, the students talked in snatches about themselves, enough so that, by the second class, Cybil had learned why each of them was there. A Hydro-Québec secretary in love with a Chilean, a woman from Roxboro whose husband had just been transferred to Florida. A businessman from Repentigny who kept repeating like a zonker, *"Soy un hombre de negocio"* each time Cybil said, *"Soy una mujer de palabras."*

One day when they were all in the cafeteria, the conversation turned to a sordid rape which had occurred the day before. The man from Repentigny confided that he had once been a Hell's Angel. He had witnessed several gang rapes, without ever taking part himself. "The girls got it pretty good. The guys didn't really know what they were doing. After a day of biking 'n' beer it took something like that to put the piss 'n' vinegar back in 'em. I can see how it wasn't any fun for the girls, though." The secretary seemed touched by the man's candour. The Roxboro woman, who hadn't understood it all, shook her head in disbelief. Cybil went to get herself a sundae, her head a turmoil of questions about these stories which, however short, always managed to tone down tensions. Any evildoer capable of telling his story with hand over heart indicating confidentiality can sidetrack the subject every time, opening the way for an emotional intimacy that leads one to "understand" the worst crimes and taste the bite of senses sharpened by violence. Told aloud, personal stories bring people together, excite ever-receptive imaginations, after which "I understand" or "it's incredible" emerges victorious, dripping saliva as if from first-hand participation in humanity.

Learning a new language was exciting to Cybil. Memorizing a vocabulary was easy. All the words had meanings and all she had to do was take a bite of them or breathe them, then suck chew and aspirate them with conviction. But when it came time to build a sentence or move into verb tenses in order to live and feel in them, the words would bolt like a run in a woman's stocking, or come and stand in gloomy chaos between her and reality.

To train her ear, Cybil began spending time in Montreal's Latino cafés and restaurants. Her ear buzzed with all the mundane and necessary phrases that ply this way and that from morn to night in everyday life. To understand, she would have to undo the semantic chain and separate the words but, too late, the sentence would have escaped in a hubbub of consonants. All that remained would be islets of meaning afloat off the coast of reality. Still, Cybil was fascinated by the almost literary dimension latent in the words *tengo, estoy, claro, que bonito, quesiera* and *corazón.* Every word she grasped through the clatter of dishes and background music sang lustily in her, its ardent resonance beating at the door of her inner self. The mind was easily carried away. Distant cities appeared, peopled with winged bipeds that bestowed new meaning on daily life. Landscapes paraded by. The foreign language was beguiling because it lent wings to faith, to a kind of hope infused by sounds which excited the imagination. These foreign words slowed the punch-drunk pace of life, rolled out the great carpet of the horizon with its sigh-inspiring colours of dawn.

"*Perdoname. ¿Puedo hacer su cuarto?*" Lost in thought, you had not heard the sound of the key in the lock. A chambermaid waits shyly for your reply. "*Si, gracias, de nada*" curls off your tongue, a melodious coil in the morning light.

5

You're sitting with Irène and Occident on one of La Recoleta's terraces. Irène wants to see everything in three days. Occident keeps saying cautiously, "Life at sea will be demanding." Around you, the foreign language props its elbows on the tables and sinks its teeth into history before lifting off like a gaily coloured hot-air balloon amid the waiters' brass trays. The conversation is lively and suddenly you hear, like a finger-snap inside you: *You're not going to write this novel. You don't have the instinct or the courage for it. Your intuition dried up with that last book. The world has changed since. The world keeps changing. From minute to minute you have to imagine elsewhere because we're already there. Almost. You've lost your sense of the present. The future has your head spinning. You're in raptures over the past. You read too much or not enough. You think keeping your distance will protect you from repeating yourself, help you understand the hidden side of your characters. Admit it, you'd like to touch bottom without dirtying yourself too much.*

You light a cigarette. Clipping an earring back in place, Irène Mage says, "Occidentally, photography . . ." In the harsh midday light, Occident's scar assumes unbearable proportions. The Hyde Park woman is back, haunting your thoughts. One hand on the dictionary, she stares into the future. There are no characters. There are too many characters.

Abruptly you stand up. "I'll be back in a minute."

A character can founder in the infinity of possibilities, create mirrors. She likes to share her loquaciousness. To steer between one word and another. She knows she mustn't muff her chance at happiness. Talking about literature is exciting to this character. She is not afraid of contradicting herself. Now and then she leans her head toward the silence. She rightfully wants to show her pink, philanthropic eyes. A character's aberrations are always impeccable. They arouse curiosity. A character sticks close to the truth the way others stay close to walls or come close to madness. She knows there's danger in looking at hurtful things. A character is a sign rescued from memory's waters. She demands a lot but insists on silence; shhh, she has to choose between desire and likelihood. The real shadow of her desire must fit over her own real shadow. She keeps tracing the same verb to be, folded back on itself like a collar around her navel. You can get close to a character. However, the proper thing to do is to look straight ahead to where death comes from. A character can shake convictions, crowd out loneliness, make the link with one's ancestors and with women who have survived the reign of men. She never tries to enfold a void, stays put where she is instead, gazing thoughtfully at the wide world out there, for the nature of the sea is such that it outlives us.

You come back to your place. The sun has heated your chair while you were gone. Occident DesRives announces that tomorrow there will be a visit to *le Tigre*. You ask who the tiger is because you don't like losing the thread. But Occident is talking now about an oceanographer, Juan, who is an octopod specialist. "He can take all three of us tomorrow, no problem."

There's a distance of three hundred metres between you and the Nuestra Señora del Pilar church cemetery. Occident pays the bill. You say, "See you later," and set off for the cemetery. In the harsh light you walk with a feeling of well-being you've never known before. Beneath the jacarandas, whose flowers you won't see and whose scent you won't smell, you think of the word austral and smile. Buenos Aires is building a love-nest in you.

You consider changing your characters' names. You walk buoyantly as if going to meet a lover and all the parts of her body you could possibly, passionately drink your fill of pleasure from.

Lighthearted. Alert. You could describe precisely every movement that brings you closer to the cemetery. All the clichés of love and death assembled at the feet of statues are bringing you back to life. You narrowly miss trampling a child. The mother glares at you with furious, very Latin eyes. At the gateway, flowers. You pass through. The word baroque comes to mind. There you are among the angels and cippi and buckets of lime. It's hot. An old lady brushes by, her small black widow's scarf touches your bare shoulder. You turn around. She's hobbling toward the gate, swallowed in the bent form of her shadow. It's hot. A workman is sweeping a myriad of white dust-specks around a burial vault. He nods to you and says, *"Mira la sepultura de Eva Perón."* You thank him. He stands aside. Two women are talking at the far end of a pathway. You walk their way. You pass them. Your presence embarrasses them. Out of the corner of your eye, you surmise that the two women, *the two women* have come together, and again together. The blue so blue of the silence suddenly confounds you like a memory lapse. The two women have disappeared.

6

Juan Existo arrives a half-hour late. He takes off his sunglasses, cries, "Occident" and gives the woman a protracted hug. The man's moustache brushes over her scar. Like a little broom, you'd say, its bristles lifting one by one over the obstacle it encounters. He blinks his eyes as if there's dust in them. He looks young but later, when you notice the wrinkled skin of his neck, you'll conclude that Occident and he are the same age.

You drive along Figuera Alcorta, past the airport parking lot. The *río* cannot be ignored, an immense brown surface that takes your breath away, that moves like a seiche across a deep lake. Juan is speaking in French. In a serious voice, he describes the economic situation, the difficult day-to-day existence of the *porteños*, the people of Buenos Aires. As you leave the city, he is conversing with Occident in Spanish. Through the wind noise, you catch the words *océano, mujer* and *futuro*. Ahead of you, light and shadow apply alternate brushstrokes across the back of Occident's neck. Grey filaments here and there through the dyed hair. Each time she turns her head toward Juan, the gold chain around her neck grazes a beauty spot. Irène draws your attention to houses made of tin and cardboard. Children dart about among languid cats on a dirt road. Farther away, glimpses of white villas framed in jade-green foliage. Because of the wind caressing your skin, you hold tight to the present. Tiger.

There is a man waiting on one of the jetties whom Juan hastens to introduce. His name escapes you, drowned in a babel of languages in which French, English and Spanish become exclamations and civilities. You board a yacht which is soon speeding across the deep-brown waters of the lagoon. Great willows sweep at you as you pass, bringing to mind those on a Louisiana bayou.

The yacht stops before an opulent white villa. Discreetly, you ask Occident the name of the man who has brought you here. James Warland is wearing white linen trousers and a short-sleeved black shirt. His arms are hairy. He offers a Chilean drink and while preparing it quotes some lines by Gabriela Mistral. In the drawing room with the walnut furniture, you recognize the strains of the Kreutzer Sonata for violin and piano. Juan asks James if he has heard from his daughter. James shrugs, pouting. Juan suggests playing some tangos for the guests. Out on the terrace, two menservants are busy preparing the *parilla*.

During the meal, Juan is lavish with praise of James Warland. Through his good offices, Juan has often obtained permission to sail in zones out of bounds to the merchant marine and the Institute's research vessel. Irène wants to know everything about Argentine history. Juan patiently answers her tourist's questions. Now and then James Warland interjects to correct a date or situate the exact site of a battle, skirmish or drought. The man is vivacious, charming, cultivated. He is clearly accustomed to conversation.

After the meal, Juan proposes a tour of the back forty. Irène and Occident accept enthusiastically. You would rather stay here and watch the dark water of the delta. "Well then," James Warland says, "I'll stay with you." He offers you a drink. You ask for a coffee. He pours himself a cognac. You settle into a big bamboo chair. Standing in front of you, the man questions you at length about Montreal and Quebec City. "It's cold there by and large, isn't it?" You're speaking in English. The man pours himself another cognac while evoking the Paris of chancelleries and the Sainte Chapelle, leaps to castles on the Rhine, then breaks off briefly to point out how like a phantom in a Nordic fable the St. Lawrence River is in winter. Without warning, except for a "by the way," the man surprises you by mentioning the October Crisis; meticulously, he explains the significance of the War Measures Act. Next you're floating with him down the Mekong. He takes you to the far corners of the earth, setting each scene with fine descriptions. You visit palaces, ruins deep in the jungle whose vegetation is growing all over the arms and faces of languorous, maleficent goddesses. You enter the great pyramid at Cheops. You pass through port cities where foreigners are blinded by the light. Entire populations rise in revolt far across the seas. You walk amid wars and revolutions, coups d'état and riots without ever seeing a drop of blood. With each new country, as if crossing a frontier, the man passes the palm of his right hand over his smooth skull.

He pours himself another drink, takes several steps toward the floating wharf, stands tall and still before the clay-laden water. He turns back to you. "Don't you think there's an odd smell? The smell of drowned bodies is so peculiar."

And suddenly he sees them. Some are wearing trousers. Their chests are lacerated. Others, completely naked, fall from the skies like flies, wrists and feet bound with wire that gouges blue furrows in their flesh. The women wear torn dresses billowing in the wind, looking like ill-omened kites. Their filthy hair is not lifted by the wind. There are dead bodies, there are live bodies. The living open their mouths as they fall from helicopters. On some days you can't see the bodies. Only plastic bags piercing the surface of the sea like nails. Underwater, the cadavers dive down among the fish. The living, whose feet alone are tied, make propellers with their arms. They soon lose consciousness, begin convulsing. An eye is a vitreous body, a white marble rolling around the bottom of the abysmal night.

You don't know at precisely what moment you thought, This man is a shark. And because he's a shark you become twice as attentive. Stimulated by your attention, he keeps saying "you know" before swallowing other words which he at once regurgitates, shorn of labials, guttural.

Now the man is pacing back and forth beside the water. You can no longer hear what he's saying. He gesticulates. Repeatedly strokes the underside of his chin as if to wipe away food remains or stop water trickling down. Perhaps you should say something but his inebriation keeps you at a distance. While he has been talking, you have gripped the arms of the chair so hard that a piece of bamboo has broken the skin on your palm between your thumb and forefinger. The falling bodies have passed very close to you. You can see the flowers and birds and love knots in the Liberty prints of the women's dresses, the three-day beards on the young men's livid cheeks, the dried sperm in the women's hair.

To calm yourself, you try now to measure that thing which is not the time a story or a spate of words or a silence takes. Evaluate the shortfall between the morality of an action, the morality of a lie, and the morality of a memory. To keep from crying, you calculate the time that awareness needs to travel the distance between the mouth which makes a statement and the eyes imprisoned in the statement. You don't know, you'd like to know, whether loquaciousness bears the seed of a repentant's morality or whether it merely accentuates a pervert's delirium.

Occident's voice. The trio approaches. James Warland recovers his wits. All that is left of his paroxysm is a tiny trickle of saliva. The man smiles broadly with all his white man's white teeth.

Irène wants to take a group picture before you leave. Everyone gathers in close ranks. You stand between Juan and Occident. The man stands at the back because of his height. There's an odd smell. Juan thanks James. A manservant accompanies the group back to the wharf.

In the car you say not a word. The man's delirium has left you mute as never before. The water of the delta is now suspect. You slip and slide in your thoughts. In a sunlit zone of water you swim peacefully enough. Suddenly he's there. He circles majestically above you. His white belly, a great massif of solid flesh, goes by like a submarine. He moves away, turns, imperturbably passes over you again, first showing a mouth that's passive, scarlike, then open, gaping enormous, a jagged vista of teeth sparkling like coral. Then the mass glides grey away. In the distance a form approaches. You recognize the

Hyde Park woman. She swims in your direction with a big knife in her teeth, or a big pen, you can't tell which. She comes toward you, hurrying to your rescue, so you think.

Back in your room you note: the novel hasn't budged an inch. Still the same one with the swollen, overworked mouth that attracts the curious in public. The Hyde Park woman is back in her place at the window. You drift aimlessly between the window and the bed. You open the drawer of the bedside table. The Bible smells mildewed. You open it at random. Laboriously you translate: "The end of all flesh is come before me; for the earth is filled with violence through them; and behold, I will destroy them with the earth." You begin again. "I have decided to put an end to all mortals on earth; the earth is full of lawlessness because of them. So I will destroy them and all life on earth." And again you try: "The loathsomeness of all mankind has become plain to me, for through them the earth is full of violence. I intend to destroy them, and the earth with them."[9]

7

Eight o'clock. A single desire stirs in you. Buenos Aires at night. You slip a city map in *Labyrinths* by Borges. The taxi deposits you at the corner of Corrientes and Montevideo. The sidewalks are swarming with people. The noise, the movement, the pollution grip you by the throat. After walking barely a hundred metres you stop at the Premier Caffe where you drink down a Coke.

Close by is the San Martin cultural centre and theatre. Faces, display cases, fragments of phrases and of culture. Behind the grand staircase, an exhibition hall. Photographs of Alicia D'Amico and Sarah Facio. Portrait photos of Latin American writers. You recognize the faces of Marquez, Fuentes, Cortázar and Borges. You discover Juan Rulfo's. Only one picture of a woman: Silvina Ocampo whose face you won't see because the woman has chosen to hide it behind a hand spreadfingered starlike, intimating keep away. The other hand is a hand that has truly gripped, a fist clenched like a scream at belly height. Below the photograph, "*Ventana donde estan los ojos.*"

In the lobby, a poster catches your eye: Danza Tango x 2. Tickets still available. The show is about to begin. A rustle of sound from the audience. The lighting follows the musicians to their instruments. From the very first notes, an unutterable feeling of here and now. A fabulous present containing all the folds of pain and solitude and happiness rolled together deep inside you, like a forgotten musical score or manuscript waiting for its moment to come. This music is part of you, a sound system that has made itself at home in you. A nervous system that irrigates your belly and entire cortex. Like feeling faint, being suddenly uprooted from reality, then subjected to the gravitational pull of a most lucid, carnal id. At each stroke of the violin bow, at each breath of the bandoneon, you dissolve in your own enigma, your yearning filled with far shores and something poignant that you cannot name.

A pair of dancers appears. The nobility of their supple, mysterious steps enchants the audience. You guess at the current of energy flowing through the cortex of each to guide those daring, leg-tangling manoeuvres. Staccato, saw-toothed beats and harmonics command each approach step and separation of the bodies, prolong the pact. Broken rhythm, broken pact. The woman turns about face, the slit of her dress opening from ankle to curve of thigh. The beauty of the coded, fetish movements where equilibrium is both unquestionably perfect and precarious.

Later, walking on Avenida Corrientes, you give way to what seems like joy. A fresh night breeze raises a creative woman's energy in you. In this city, you exist. Energy alone is double in you.

8

Today, the day after that *porteñas* night, Cybil Noland can almost touch the energy circulating in the room. *Tonight, Sixtine, I came close to you. I let myself be swept away by desire, that old word we cheat with sometimes so we can forget how fast everything goes and how one day we'll have no ideas left to put between ourselves and the universe.*

A message has been slipped under your door: mission preparation meeting at one o'clock in the hotel lobby.

A whole light-filled morning free. Take off down a long street bordering Las Heras Park. At the corner of Santa Fe and Coronel Díaz, the pollution gets in your eyes with sick-dog jaundiced airs. You take refuge briefly in the red décor of the Tolón Café. Before long you resume a delectable stroll in the Sunday-out-for-walking light.

Little by little the neighbourhood reveals itself. Shop windows offer unembellished necessities in this concrete and brick milieu. On the heaved and broken sidewalks, men argue in front of their stalls where tomatoes and zucchini, apples and bananas glow in primary colours. Children, vendors of roses. On Salguero Street near Soler, the Freud Video Club poster makes you smile. A little farther on you stop, incredulous, outside the Café Freud. Children play among the palms in Guémez Square. Like a mirage, another sign, another café, this one named Jung. A splendrous church dominates the square. Its bells are ringing. Women are selling palm fronds as in the days of your childhood.

For a minute or two you're walking with your little hand in the soft hand of Maman Noland. She's wearing her flesh-pink dress all covered with flowers. The bells of Mary Queen of the World are ringing for all they're worth. Suddenly there's no cultural distance any more. Everything coincides. The churches are filled to bursting, the women are mothers, the men play at being fathers, one child equals one child. The family is a family. The young women have fiancés and are brides-to-be. The men wear the pants. As in your childhood, everything is in order, thanks to God.

And yet, walking between the churches, schools and convents of your childhood, you used to drag your feet and stray from the beaten path whenever you could. A double time was already embedding itself in you, a kind of convex reality through which you could see where the future was coming from. You made the most of the future because it was possible back then to make exultant leaps in history and change its course. Then the churches emptied, the convents closed. The family ceased to be a cell. Now the fiancées were future lovers. Turbulence. Youthful exuberance and readiness to try anything. With your eyes fixed on the horizon, you learned to thumb your nose at the past and look women in the eye. And on this sunny Palm Sunday, the days of things past are back to skulk around in your mind again, the last thing you wanted.

Back to now.

You enter the church as the priest is preachifying. He keeps saying *mujer* and *mujeres*. You finally get the gist. Ah yes, the adulterous woman. The faithful listen religiously on both sides of the main aisle. In his gold-embroidered chasuble, the man mouths dire forebodings. Oremus.

You buy a newspaper and sit down at a table in the Café Freud. At neighbouring tables, people are reading, talking, scribbling, each in whichever fashion trying to ennoble daily life. Writing: that way of resting the forearm on the table, holding the pen between thumb and forefinger. Sighs between one paragraph and the next; when things have reached an impasse, that way of running a hand through the hair, stroking the chin, lifting impassioned eyes to passersby who have other things on their minds. And suddenly this image: terraces in all the great cities are occupied by women writing, oblivious to the wind and weather, and to the paper that indiscriminately blots up meritorious ideas, evil thoughts, declarations of love, grocery lists and pure fiction conceived that very moment.

The journal *Pagina 12*. Page 43, a photograph of Nicole Brossard. A brief announcement of a talk she is to give this evening at the Feria del Libro. You had forgotten the meeting. You arrive late. Occident is dressed all in black. On her head a cap of the kind worn by young and less young consumers the world over. Irène has put on spiral earrings. Occident talks library and virtual reality but you hear none of it, excited at the thought of seeing Brossard again. Later, you ask Irène to go with you to the Book Fair. With her camera, of course.

9

The exhibition hall is immense. The publishers' information booths are staffed by hostesses whose miniskirts are
undoubtedly effective for boosting readers' purchasing
power. You ask directions several times before locating the
Pizarnik Room where you find yourselves seats in the third
row, hoping to be noticed by the novelist. The audience is
Latin feminine except for a handful of men from the British
embassy. The translator is introduced, who in turn introduces
Brossard. A nice complicity develops between the two
women. Brossard speaks with as much conviction as ever. She
has aged a bit. Her eyes are bright.

"... because we are exiled from ourselves in the language
and imagery of our respective cultures, we cannot make spontaneous use of these indispensable tools of self- and world-
awareness. To a certain degree, we are forced to elucidate our
insufferable position in the midst of conceptualizations that
reflect our exclusion and fragmentation, in the midst of con-
tradictions that are not ours but for which we must pay, and

which engulf us in ambivalence, double-binds, guilt, self-doubt, self-censorship. It will avail us nothing to raise our voices if by so doing we reinforce the landscapes of the status quo. It is through Man's fiction that we have become fictional. Let us emerge from fiction through fiction. We shall exist in the story we are about to invent, but we shall need towering rages, a will more preposterous than any surrealistic desire, curiosity that leads us to commit terrible indiscretions and persevere with arduous inquiries. We must learn to push beyond limits."

Brossard's words have revived old anxieties. The questions are back, emerging like those bare rocks lying in wait before Barnabé Island the previous spring. You like Brossard's straightforward talk and vitality. You yourself remain worried, assailed by doubts, groping for a point of view that might make humanity lovable. Now that reality and fiction bear out *ex aequo* our tribulations and boldest dreams as well, you keep hoping your intricate schemes will help keep literature from falling into disuse.

The translator asks if there are any questions. There are several. With each optimistic reply from Nicole, you dismiss the dangerous thought that words are flat like stick-on estrogen and testosterone patches that artificially prolong the pro-creative drive. After a time, you imagine yourself with a knee on the ground and a foot in the block, tense, keyed-up like a long-distance runner waiting for the starting gun. Oh yes, those words that keep coming to your rescue are terribly alive.

After the talk, Irène will take several pictures of the two of you. Nicole will put her hand on your shoulder. You'll smile, the corners of your mouth aquiver. Later, you'll all go to join some Argentinian novelists in a restaurant on La Placita. Privately, you'll confide to Nicole that, yes, you have this double-time feeling, a feeling of double *telling* that fills you with indescribable anxiety. Callously, she will dismiss your distress, saying that each woman must face the test of the telling alone, "I mean to say the difficult part. We must get used to the idea that a well-written sentence will never camouflage the moronic look it gives one to think that one can get the better of death; *so strap creative energy around your waist like a safety belt and forget about fear.*"

You would like her to set sail with all of you aboard the *Symbol*.

Back at the Hotel Alvear, Irène takes you to the bar. This is your first tête-à-tête since the inky night you spent together in Rimouski.

Irène orders champagne. From the first sips, she seems bent on conquering the world. She talks volubly while looking over your shoulder. A torrid quality to what she's saying. Every word smoulders. Wanting everything, the present, the contrary, and most of all to leave her mark. "I'd like . . . and it goes to my head whenever I produce. My passion for light breeds too many images." Reality. Her hands move continually in the smoky air, describing the same motif which you hasten to qualify as digital. You think, "she's running off at the mouth" because you don't see the image, only her feeling as a lonesome thing in the foreground of her excitement. What she is saying is incoherent, perfectly intelligible, totally moving and abstract.

When she's on her second glass of champagne and you've given up thought of stopping her, lo and behold she brings out her silence as others do an argument. Like a ribbon of nostalgia, the silence undulates in the air-conditioned atmosphere and buzz of the bar.

Without looking at you, without moving her eyes, she takes your hand. Her palm is warm as if it has sheltered a small animal or lived a long closed-fisted life deep in an otter coat. You hypothesize that the hand is warm because Irène is an artist and you've heard her say, like Clarice Lispector, "I try to photograph the fragrance." The warmth of this hand shelters your own world of fantasy. The warmth penetrates your novelist's body and you dare not move in sight of your character.

THE *DARK* FUTURE

"Nobody laughs in a dream."

– HERMAN BROCH

"At times I don't care a bit if I never touch reality."

– FRANCE THÉORET

THE *SYMBOL*

They had been aboard the *Symbol* for three hours now. Juan Existo had come with them to La Plata, where they had threaded their way among the stevedores and sailors on the wharves. Some Argentinian sailors were to join the crew of the *Symbol*. With their wives they formed a noisy little gathering from which these affectionate Apollo butterflies were escaping the women's hands to light on the heads of men or flutter against a cheek, faces turned already toward the sea. Some of the sailors held fiancées about the waist and others tenderly squeezed the necks of tearful brides. Amid the tears, exclamations and wet kissy onomatopoeias, the three women were the targets of suspicious glances thrown by the "better halves." "Every time we board it's the same scene," Occident explained. "The women imagine things. . . ."

Captain Carlos Loïc Nadeau had greeted them in his lilting "symphonic" accent composed of the sensitive, mixed notes attributable to a plural origin, which in his case had become confused over the years with the term "oddity." He introduced his first officer, Jean Lanctôt; the ship's doctor, Thomas Lemieux, a tall, nervous man with bushy eyebrows; the cook, Paul Blanquette of Baie-Saint-Paul; and the chaplain, *Padre* Pedro Sinocchio, a bony little man with gentle, anxious eyes who never opened his mouth without running his forefinger round his roman collar, as though there were a cause-and-effect relationship between speaking and a stylishly visible Adam's apple. The student with the earring whom Cybil had observed at Rimouski was along too. Occident introduced him: Derrick Tremblay. The man was thinner. At twilight the divers appeared: Pascal, Robert alias Flash, and Philippe Demers.

The ship cast off. Everybody waved, on principle for some, with feeling for others. Cybil had an urge to laugh and talk loudly, to dance and run about, in short to exist so physically that there wouldn't be anything else to think about but a sequence of acts and their solution of continuity throughout a life.

When the sun had set and the horizon had turned to ink sprinkled with stars, Cybil went up on deck. With her hair streaming in the wind, leaning on her lingo, she let La Sixtine and her story come her way. She was possessed by such strong conviction regarding the constellations and the boundless universe that on her lips a taste even stronger than her taste for travel mingled with the salty sea air, which inexplicably always excites the body's fluid mass.

That night she fell asleep with one eye on the porthole and high expectations for things to come.

THE LIBRARY

On the first morning, Irène turned up at Cybil's doorstep in a lather.

"Occident insists we spend the first five days in the library. She says we have to do research. I protested. She repeated, 'I insist, it's necessary,' and made me promise to do as she said. I don't know what argument or charm I yielded to, but I promised! She sent me to get the same commitment from you."

Cybil thought she was dreaming. She asked Irène to repeat what she had said. In the space of a few seconds, fear, anger and desperation in turn swept through all her neurons and she declared war on Occident.

"But there's the sea. The wind, the colour of the sky, the power of our senses. That's what we're going to need to produce this book. We have to be free to move around. Breathe normally. Eat, sing. Talk and laugh. We can't shut ourselves up in a library in the name of art. We're here to open our eyes. So we can feel the sun heating our blood and the salt air parching our lips. We're here so our bodies and minds can give way to the wind and the silence and the night. We're here to let our imaginations float free."

"She says that mealtimes spent with her, the captain, the chaplain and the doctor will do amply to put us in the picture."

"She's crazy!" Cybil said, snatching open the cabin door. Derrick Tremblay was waiting for them just outside. The women demanded he explain what was going on. The only answer he would give was "I would prefer not to."[10] Several corridors to walk through. Doorlatch. The library.

Tiny but attractive. Large illustrated books on one side. Other books and magazines on the other. A card table in the middle. Four chairs as for a game of bridge. At the far end, the placid eye of a porthole. On the walls, portraits of sea captains. Engravings. Ships and end-of-the-world tempests.

The two women go instinctively to the porthole as though it has qualities to make them think freedom. Soft light, a few whitecaps on the same dark brown water. Without speaking, they inspect the bookshelves: three Bibles, the complete set of Jacques Cousteau books full of pictures, a biography of the diver Jacques Mayol; Victor Hugo, Jules Verne, Herman Melville and Joseph Conrad novels. Technical books on core sampling and deep-sea fishing. *Amantes marines* by Robert Choquette, *Portulan* by Pierre Perrault, *Les fous de Bassan* by Anne Hébert. Mixed in with scientific magazines, some issues of *Playboy* and *Penthouse*.

"It's a bad joke!"

"A kidnapping, you mean."

"I don't think so. Something tells me Occident doesn't want to scare us off. Make us behave, perhaps, stir up some introductive turmoil in us. With Occident, nothing's left to chance."

"We shouldn't have been so trusting. Would you be brave enough to trash the library in protest?"

"No."

"Would you seduce Occident as a last resort?"

"No."

Irène has planted herself at the porthole. With her thumbs and forefingers she frames some invisible subjects, divides the horizon into imaginary segments in the bright light. Cybil paces back and forth, hunts for a pen, something to write with. Something to write. Visual images and hypotheses jostle in her head.

At half-past noon, Derrick Tremblay brought some sandwiches and chips, a jug of water and some coffee. He said, "Time is a thing that's hard to gauge. I envy you for all the time you have before you." Around two o'clock, Cybil decided to leaf through a book of pictures. Corals, abyssal plains, great ocean ridges. In a garden of inky darkness, thousands of living organisms waiting for a nourishing rain of carcasses and refuse. The big female anglerfish appeared, followed by the great sea-serpent and the batfish with red lips, arousing Cybil briefly. Irène came and sat beside her.

"When all's said and done, this is going to force us to compare our impressions."

"Yes, it's going to be our *camera lucida*."

She pictured Irène in her darkroom, moving from one pan to the next, lifting out big sheets become suddenly meaningful and valuable under the infra-red light. In the name of light, braving the darkness of acid solitude.

As if struck by an impeccable idea, Irène touches Cybil's arm and exclaims, "Tomorrow I'll bring my Nikon!" Then, in a voice of defeat, "Oh, I forgot – Occident doesn't allow paper or pencil. She says it all has to be done through memory and imagination."

"No camera, then."

"Yes, my 'digital.' So once back in Montreal I can recompose everything. Take apart, reframe and remake the evidence of our time at sea. Who knows what I'll turn you into, what unsuspected picture of you my whimsy will bring out. The book's future is hidden in my camera."

"The future is not an appearance of appearance."

At five o'clock the door opened and they were led to their cabins. Later, a sailor took them to the dining room.

SIBYLS AND *IGNUDI*

They're there around the table. Sitting straight and proud, pleased with themselves. Occident is wearing a sundress of the same turquoise her office walls are painted. For the first time, she has put makeup on the scar. Cybil has barely set foot in the dining room before the double-time feeling takes hold and the gusts of terrible words and meaning she has lined up to declare war on Occident vanish in the aroma of the soup.

The chaplain says grace in Latin. The captain, whose duty is to initiate conversation, observes that this sea is reassuringly calm compared with the mouth of the St. Lawrence, where it bares its hellcat's claws at the drop of a hat. *Padre* Sinocchio likes to be courteous and affable. He would like to say a few words about artistic life in Quebec. He gropes for a name to start off with but can't find it, so in embarrassment settles for talking about His Eminence Paul-Émile Léger, whom he had the honour of meeting once in Rome. Occident leaps at the chance to haul everyone inside the Sixtine Chapel, which she knows like the back of her hand.

With sweeping gestures, she undertakes to describe what can be seen perfectly from the vantage point of the celebrant, can barely be seen at all from visitor positions, and can be conceived in different ways besides. Here, the *ignudi* merely provide punctuation; up there, the narration unfolds in a way that deceives expectations. Today the same discourse on the creation of the world would be unthinkable because according to the rules of narrative you have to point at infinity with one hand and exploit it with the other.

Then she gave a commentary on "The Parting of the Waters," "The Creation of the Stars" and "The Separation of Light and Shadow." Cybil wanted to break in but Occident ignored her and kept talking.

"Yes, they're pagan and there are five of them, from Persia, Libya, Eritrea, Cumae and Delphi. Each faces a Hebrew prophet. Each holds a book in her hand, except for the youthful Delphic sibyl who is holding the rolled end of a papyrus scroll. Her eyes are turned to the left, drawn by the camera we would say, or perhaps a director's voice. Her lips are parted. The Libyan sibyl, all curves and rotundity, looks away from a big book she's holding open in a V in front of her. The Eritrean with muscular arms is preparing to turn the page of a book on a lectern behind her. Her body could be a young man's. The Persian sibyl, an elderly woman clad head to foot in ample folds of drapery, is holding a book very near her face, scrutinizing it eagerly. The body of the sibyl of Cumae, who is of menopausal age, is all knolls and mounds. Her bare right arm is as muscular as God's. Supposably long-sighted, she reads holding a book well away and down at waist level, as if to differentiate it from her person. Her face is hard, her nose aquiline, her chin pointed.

"Since all these women share association with a book, I'll leave the floor now to Cybil."

For the moment, nothing to add.

At which point *Padre* Sinocchio hastened to assert – you could tell he was asserting from the crimson flush of his cheeks – that the flood phenomenon could not be denied. Noah, the Ark and all that could not be merely the fruit of our imaginations.

"You know," said the doctor, "today the flood would be inconceivable. We have enough scholars, engineers and computers to pull us through the flood."

"Yes, but chaos is still with us," Cybil put in with the verve of a she-wolf.

The doctor muttered some misanthropic observations and then fell silent, thinking that this woman who claimed to write novels belonged to another age. Which one?

Irène's knee touched Cybil's leg and Cybil, driven suddenly by an unfamiliar mechanism, felt a pressing urge to declare, *"Nobody knows what lies in the human body."*

"Only the lonely," Lemieux replied with a smile.

Then bedlam set in, language behaving like a certified crackpot starved for dreams. Surrounded by these fictional characters, it gulped down everything, all stories great and small, rapidly and with relish. Insatiable, it lifted the film of solitude that gives protection from others and siphoned out everything unwritable, unsharable. We would have to learn to handle the abstract, anxious side of language to enable reality to pass the thread of time through the eye of the needle, to enable fleeting expressions and conventional words to become currents of thought. Language was spinning uncontrolled like a hurricane, a waterspout. Language was drinking a flood of its own making. We would have to give language a lot of love to have it exhilarate us without drowning us in the chaotic spate of words our bodies keep telling us they want more of. We would have to woo it ardently to have it point us toward the future, with open arms forming a great avenue of blue spruces perfumed by the earth at its best.

Language accompanied the whole length of this first meal. It wound around the broad shoulders of Carlos Loïc Nadeau when he talked of discipline and authority. It made *Padre* Sinocchio even thinner, destroyed his credibility and left him limp and ill at ease behind his roman collar. It slipped inside the spirals of Irène's earrings, pinched the lobes of her ears, made her vigilant for misleading, over-exposed visual images.

Language is merciless, Cybil thought. For a word misplaced or a phrase too many, it will destroy reputations. Nor will it forgive being ignored or courted absentmindedly.

Language must be turned toward the future, forced to bring light to the humblest corners of cities, led gradually to reveal the underside of the lunacies of exile, memory and ambition by which reasonable beings are consumed.

Language filters thoughts, flirts with our weaknesses, then, as necessary, justifies all – playful, psychotic and logical alike.

Padre Sinocchio strove to gather up the snatches of conversation, the scattered determinations floating untidily about the dining room. He blinked his eyes and swallowed too quickly, swept up in the flood of fast, superficial visual images which nevertheless would never shape up beside the New Testament. He would have liked to suggest that there be more praying in the face of the wind and the dangers arising from the sea.

Carlos Loïc Nadeau spoke to him in slow cadences. Ever the charmer, the captain held it essential to caress the sea while navigating since each caress is worth at least one prayer, and with caresses and understanding of their magic one could get what one wanted from the sea, even though things went wrong sometimes.

Simultaneously, the doctor and Irène each lit a cigarette. Cybil looked Occident straight in the eye as if about to inundate her with ferocious, unpunctuated questions. Occident looked downward, then toward Paul Blanquette who was approaching ceremonially, sparkling with joie de vivre and bearing a big silver platter where, steeping in its juices, was the mysterious duck in Mornay sauce for which he was famous.

Language stirred an anxiety in Cybil that was near absurd and she could find nothing to say but, "We live in a mad world."

"It were ever thus," Doctor Lemieux replied promptly. He abhorred the thought that learned women could say stupid things. "It were ever thus. Do you think that existential angst began with you, Mademoiselle Noland? Surely you agree that men have known since long ago that the secret of life is proportionate to the angst Man suffers. Living right is strictly a matter of science. Just as there's a science of the sea, there's a science of human misfortune. Living right supposes that one has lived and reflected sufficiently to have made a science of this misfortune. One must learn about simple things like hunting, copulation and war before imagining that the secret of life lies in something like love for one's neighbour. And equality – let's not even mention that. When you say we live in a mad world, you're showing in a crude way that you're incapable of understanding and describing a form of natural chaos."

Cybil did not reply. Lemieux belonged to another age. Which one?

"The sea enriches everyone's soul," Sinocchio ventured. "In fact, we've known since the flood that we must keep looking for the first dove."

Irène sipped at her wine. Occident had completely lost face. With one hand she seemed to be trying to protect the doctor against all life's vicissitudes and with the other she was re-arranging the captain's eating utensils so that he really would only have to lift a finger in order to eat.

Padre Sinocchio opened his mouth again to speak but his forefinger "djammed" like a foreign word between his starched collar and the flesh of his neck, which would never feel the scented delight of a well-loved woman's silky hair.

Irène burst out laughing, so loudly and uncontrollably that two sailors appeared as though an emergency had been declared. Cybil fell into a fathomless reverie. Waterless. Horizonless. Lawless. She fell headfirst like a rocket fired upside down in a strange world in which familiar questions seemed suddenly to have no foundation.

Thomas Lemieux picked up his knife, shook his head, thinking better of it, and drew from his pocket a handsome silver case, out of which he took a silver scalpel.

"Ladies, open your eyes. You will soon be given to see how fresh meat parts under the scalpel of science. When you have finished with the library and have come up on deck to breathe the real air of life at sea, I promise you a fine performance. Bear in mind that we must never lose our footing, whether we're cast in concrete or caged by the tides of misfortune."

PARKS

The following day, Cybil and Irène went on their own to the library. Irène had brought her Nikon. Cybil sat down with Victor Hugo's *L'homme qui rit*. Leafing through the book, she came upon the passage describing the various monarchist clubs to be found in London after the Restoration of Charles II; since she could not write, she memorized. One was the She Romps Club. A woman would be seized in the street, a city woman who happened to be passing, the least old and ugly possible; she would be dragged forcibly into the club and made to walk on her hands with her feet in the air and her face hidden by her downward-hanging skirts. If she did it with ill grace, what was not hidden would be lashed a mite with a riding whip. It would be her own fault. The riders in this kind of riding ring were called "the jumpers." There were also the Uglymen's Club, the Beefsteak Club, the Splitfarthing Club, the Hot Flashes Club, the Hellfire Club, the Great Mohock Club and the Fun Club, which Cybil judged to be the ancestor of the sadistic and vandalish gang in the film *Clockwork Orange*.

Disgusted, she took a look at *Les travailleurs de la mer*. She went with Gilliatt to the bottom of the abyss, she watched him battle the maleficent octopus, the fictional monster of the day, then, as the man was about to free Clubin's skeleton from beneath the crabs, she closed the book.

When she came back up to the surface, Irène was waiting, camera trained in her direction. Cybil said, "I'll cry out." Irène heard, "I'll create." She pressed the button at the moment Cybil's lips broadened into a smile at the *cr* in "I thought creation was crucial."

For a while Irène moved around Cybil taking close-ups of her eyes and mouth, where words might more readily be taken as sincere. Then, thinking that someone on this earth must look like Cybil, she asked if Cybil had ever procreated. "Procreated, brought forth, given life, had a baby, answer me!" Since Cybil remained silent, Irène announced that she was grandmother to a five-year-old girl who would soon be starting school. Cybil looked at her in astonishment. A soothing tenderness dawned between the two women. And together they drifted, slowly, very slowly, each letting herself be borne by her childhood and by those little fluffy white clouds which to an affectionate and tidy mother represent years gone by.

Now the two Montrealers seize on all the memories from upstream of adulthood, when one of them became a woman of visual images and the other a woman of words.

Sitting face to face, they unwrap the names of streets, parks and schools as if they are precious gifts, then deposit them in the middle of the table so they can be counted and shared. A private dialogue.

Irène offers first of all a hazy picture of Belmont Park. As in the earliest daguerreotypes, there remains not a trace of humanity. Gone are all signs of life with its merry-go-round movement. Finally the picture comes into focus and this time there's laughing and bustle and shouting for joy among the booths and rides. Suddenly there she is, the mechanical fat woman, Belmont Park's laughing fat woman who laughs so hard and so long she can really frighten you. She always fascinated the child Irène with her long breaths of uncontrollable and absolutely amazing hahs cascading waterfall-fashion down her ample breast. An enormous laugh that shook that body full of folds and hees and hos and fat round her arms. A greedy laugh that swelled her cheeks with some mysterious wind and seemed to come from under her tongue, a tiny organ playing in her joyful ogress face. A full laugh offered free to children, who would go away saying, "The lady's crazy," or ask uneasily, "Moman, is it us the fat lady's laughing at?"

Belmont Park scintillates in the middle of the table and the girls take three roller-coaster rides. Her head spinning, Cybil suspends time so as to catch her breath, then plays the Lafontaine Park card. Once she has the pond in her thoughts, she invites Irène to climb into a green rowboat. They sit side by side and row slowly because the grey wooden oars are heavy, but also because the sun and the lapping of the water are wakening a springtime drowsiness in them. The reflection of the sun off the water intrigues Irène, who wants to know if they can stop time so she can capture the sun's reflection and her own at the same time. The same time that words are feeling out these things, so far away and beautiful amid the greenery, like a peaceful day in childhood.

Being there, there again, and agreeing to take the bus up to Mount Royal. Picnicking on the broad grassy slope overlooking Beaver Lake and the Chalet, with people walking all around, holding leashes, in pace with their dogs. On the lake, mallard ducks and swans swim about among the dragonflies and waterstriders. While eating her sandwich, each adds something to the memory. Soon the table is filled with small objects: chewing gum, wax crayons, rabbit's feet for the good luck and happiness one has to attend to from morn till night if one wants to grow up.

Talking about the many objects that clutter people's lives brings the two women to the first books they read, firing them with such pleasure that they decide to do another round of parks, this time as adults. Irène heads for the Luxembourg Gardens. Cybil goes to walk in Hyde Park beside the Serpentine.

Irène walks along the terrace where the queens of France stand guard. She comments as she goes: "A lewd pelvic tilt from Clémence Isaure, a *nasty* look from Louise de Savoye, a seductive pose by Marguerite d'Angoulême. Valentine de Milan holds a book. Anne de Beaulieu's foot peeks from under her dress like a small rodent. I worry for Anne of Austria, whose left hand is withered by the years. Now I stand before Sainte Clothilde and I'll go no farther. Her face is so beautiful and contemporary it makes me want to talk to her of love and photography till she's as real as another real live woman upon this earth."

To this Cybil replies, "All I can see is leaves and greenery, and a *grumpaholic* crossing a path. A woman in a long red coat is resting on the grass. Now she's looking my way. Her eyes are made up Egyptian fashion."

Irène cuts in, saying, "Look, here are the names of trees you'll find in the gardens. Listen, I'll read them for you, you might want to use them as background some day. Here I go: sycamore maple, sweet chestnut, silver linden, mulberry, lotus, ginko and paulownia, Siberian elm, Atlas cedar."

The word Atlas sets Cybil orbiting the planet. The urge to write comes on strong, as muscular as a seductive woman who wants to take her to bed, who would touch her spine lightly at atlas level, murmuring in a foreign tongue fiery words that would open the door to a thousand interpretations. The caress would continue, tracing words all the way down Cybil's spine. By concentrating, Cybil can feel the roundness of the finger, its pressure, the pace at which one letter leads to another, the pauses that stand for punctuation. Can feel the warmth of the woman's finger through her skin, Gothic letters, ornamental capitals, graceful italics making senses and sememes of plea-sure on her skin. Then the other pressing her whole body against Cybil's. With a single sigh, breasts, belly, thighs flood Cybil's cortex. Burning lips unbridled on her neck.

Since this has lasted some time, Cybil has leaned her head back over the backrest of her chair. As naturally as can be, the light stirs her lashes on its way to her iris, seeking its due in colours and images. When she opens her eyes, Irène is sitting by her side with a smile, watching the shaken novelist.

Five o'clock came. Derrick Tremblay took them back to their respective cabins. At supper time, language as she is spoke took over around the table and each diner showed increasing obses-sion with a specialty, be it God, discipline, science, or a longing for water and the sea where hope springs eternal.

ETCHINGS

The following day. Light pours over the etchings on the walls. The engravings emerge from their anonymity, awaken feeling.

Horrendous seas. The wave-lashed sides of dangerously heeling ships. Near sinking. Men with biceps swollen like huge nerves roll wide terror-stricken eyes at the monstrous sea-serpents and their spume. Others lift their eyes to heaven, clinging to the shrouds, will-o-the-wisps in the sombrous mass of the sea and darkness. Suspended between the sea and the heavens, a captain, his body frozen in improbable stance, imperturbably defies the terrifying mass heaving beneath his ship, his law, his science.

Torment. Movement. Torsion. Tumult. Such great and muscular, secular effort. Before nature's fury, man resists, mingling his vanity with the unspeakable tumult of the waves. A hideous fate glows lyrical among the breakers buffeting the ominous O's of mouths distorted by anguish and panic.

Tall masts, dream-haunted shafts, rise amid the turmoil of the wind; libido feeds voraciously on the darkness and grey-tint effects obtained at the time of inking; and the world appears as a vast spectacle of signs that give each era its aesthetics, depending on its fears, beliefs, and vanities in the figurative sense.

Cybil was thinking that the diversity of aesthetics was now so great that one would have to devote hours of silence and observation to interpreting them. There were too many feelings, too many bodies of knowledge. Too many signs. Too much of the same kind of life, with creatures of all shapes and descriptions coming into the present out of the sea, then out of the forest and the desert, like powerful symbols responsible for providing background to men's imaginations as they toiled toward cities by dint of narrative and new tools. Skin had been tatooed and tanned, heads crowned, skulls collected, bones carved for game-playing, counting, decorating and wounding. The narrative had turned women into blobs of *mirth*stery and fertility, then into silent prey, then into sun-tanned, electrical things that turned on big-city passersby. All this time, the sexes of men were being carved to point straight at the sky, imploring God to do the dirty work of cleansing women's sexes of all impurities so that sons could step over the present and ride off on the stars. Bestiary. The aesthetics of roaring storms. Surf.

In the morning light, Cybil absentmindedly drew the back of her hand across the table. This raised an immense breaker you would think straight out of a Hokusai engraving. The wave hung aesthetic and menacing over Cybil. Then, lost and adrift in the reiterant eternity of waves, she tumbled and whirled until the image transformed into the smooth, turquoise water of a California swimming pool in which La Sixtine was swimming, waiting for the novelist to arrive.

No words at all that day, for deep inside her the thundering of the sea, the tumult of the waters, the astonishing effect of these old engravings had to be calmed.

THE CHARACTER

It was the last night before real life on deck would resume. Occident had promised. For the first time, Cybil was hearing the creaking of the ship and feeling its movement. Her hand was shaking and she thought some mysterious fever must be about to carry her off. A tango was playing in the cabin next door.

She wrote all night long, roaming the sun-filled streets of the city armed to the teeth. Displaced in time and space, La Sixtine appeared in San Telmo Square, her eyes closed and the wind in her hair, playing one age-old tango after the other: *"Sus ojos se cerraron," "Volio una noce," "Silencio."* Men are dancing together, improvising rapid step sequences. They change partners frequently, the gnarled hand of one taking the place of another's calloused palm. Their hats shade their foreheads. They wear wide-legged pants and now and then their rumpled jackets billow in the wind as they spin. Now comes the time for mothers to dance together. Their breasts, sore from repeated nursings, touch painfully and after only a few exuberant patterns they lose heart for dancing. Other neighbourhood women in white Sunday dresses replace them. They are quickly reminded of their roles as exiles; reluctantly, they give up their places, this time to women who are exemplary dancers, while Cybil strolls from city to fiction with La Sixtine on her arm, among the dykes, *sills* and pillow-lavas of the great Atlantic deeps.

Cybil puzzled all night, trying to understand the ties that bound her to La Sixtine and those she enjoyed with Irène. Perhaps that's what writing fiction does for us, it shows us what binds us to beloved imaginary beings with passion and sheer delight, as though about to lose our own identity, gain in humanity, increase the fleshly significance of the universe.

Each time, we must get close to our character, share her anxieties and joys. Impossible to let her go free as the wind, exempt from angst. Her anxiety should be exemplary. We must make her a cradle and also a coffin that fit. In between, find her an apartment and water the African violets on her balcony so that passersby will notice how pretty it all looks; dress her, sift through her life, get her out of scrapes, watch her dig her future surrounded by wars and religions. Sometimes the character might give birth to another character, catching us off guard so we think of letting reality do its thing and sometimes even our own story. Standing at the window, undoing her hair, opening her mail or a drawer or her inmost thoughts, the character is never through with existence. As a subject of inquiry, she lets herself be reached more readily from childhood on, because this is always more or less where she begins growing up. Then superstitions and big know-it-all super-egos hovering and circling like so many vultures make her cry. Where she screams, we must not touch her even lightly.

Characters, displace my death, displace the wind, redouble your fervour so that language, humble and fertile as it is, may rely on you who enjoy impunity.

THE SHARK

As chance would have it, the first person Cybil met on this first day of light, sea and wind was *Padre* Sinocchio. The man had swapped his cassock for white linen trousers and a black T-shirt. His eyes shone with pleasure at seeing Cybil.

"Mademoiselle Noland! I'm told you're writing a novel about Buenos Aires. I'm so happy!"

Four paces away, his upper body slightly bent toward Cybil, *Padre* Sinocchio gives an impression of being in the pulpit. Cybil has one hand on the companionway rail, a leg half bent and a foot poised to mount from one step to the next. Between the *padre*'s legs she sees Irène and Occident in deep discussion on deck. Slightly beyond, the divers form a trefoil-shaped mass against a dazzling blue background. The doctor is in front of them. He is seated on a wooden crate, bending over a metal table. In his hand he holds a scalpel on which the sunlight glints with a thousand fires. Morse. Morsel.

Cybil is about to say a word or two to correct the *padre*'s misconception but the man ploughs on.

"Buenos Aires, or Argentina I should say, boasts magnificent examples of baroque style, the cathedrals of Córdoba and Buenos Aires, the churches of Santa Catalina, La Campanila. Ah, the baroque, a feast for the eyes! Mademoiselle Noland, did you know that 'baroque thought taken as a whole, actuated by a yearning for Paradise Lost (according to Ors), hesitates between Chaos and Cosmos'?[11] Hyperboles, metaphors, a taste for infinity – you will never know boredom if you heed your baroque heart. And you will learn of the role played by the Company of Jesus in the spread of this architecture. The Company, you know, gave the world two famous architects: Martellange and Derand. The number of churches sponsored by the Jesuits is astonishing."

At what moment may a priest be said to be Jesuitical? Cybil imagines the man bare-chested and tied to a tree deep in a Quebec forest. A necklace of burning hot stones hangs about his neck. Where the stones touch him, the skin rises, blistered, ready to burst out like an identity. There is a buzzing of black flies and mosquitos; at his feet, well-trampled ferns, clover and weeds. Fog rolls over the martyr. Then he reappears, this time with wrists bound together and held over his head by an iron hoop. Gold hoops hang from the extremity of each nipple. Lips, nostrils and eyebrows, navel and testicles – the man is pierced everywhere. Before him stands a hulk of a man partly clad in black leather. The latter is wrapped in thought, mentally calculating the pressure the weights must exert for the pain to seep slowly under the other's armpits then suddenly penetrate the muscles and bones of the thorax, raising his sex high so its shadow will spurt like an experience of the limits to which, they say, man likes to cultivate his pain like an art.

Cybil banishes the image with a shake of her head, but *Padre* Sinocchio's mouth keeps fabricating syllables, on and on, eagerly circling his god of deliverance with all imaginable baroque torments.

On deck, Occident and Irène are talking to the divers. Cybil joins them, relieved to have escaped Sinocchio's enthusiasm and particularly the morbid images it has raised. Dressed in white, ill-shaven, Thomas Lemieux is preparing to open the belly of a small, freshly caught, freshly dead white shark, its jaws a string of prayer teeth. He looks hard at Cybil. A drop of sweat falls into the shark's eye.

"The hand that holds the scalpel must always excite the imagination. The shark is said to be indestructible. Brutal, greedy, bloodthirsty and predatory. Michelet called it *the beautiful devourer of nature, a genuine devourer.* Which is why, whether blue, white, grey or tiger, it is frequently compared to man. Quick to move in on flesh, its mouth often red with the blood of its victims, the shark fascinates."

Lemieux continues, cutting off discussion. " *'Every scholar is a little bit cadaver,'* Victor Hugo said. Dissection is an activity of the mind like philosophy or criticism. When I was a student, I loved the smell of ether and those long sessions when I would bend over cadavers and learn to wield my instruments, cutting carefully into those spaces the professor called, depending on his mood, wells of agitation, gentle cavities, vertiginous canals, fatal gorges, or chasms of resistance. For a long time I allowed myself to be lulled by this man's voice. He was not much older than my classmates. I recognized myself in his bright, anguished eyes; I could learn from history, dialogue with death, get close to suffering. He judged all cadavers by the firmness or flabbiness of their bellies;

herein lay the whole measure of differences. He made no distinction between the sexes or races. For him there was belly and non-belly. He used no antonyms. The faces and sexes of the cadavers were always covered with a sheet. 'Belly is belly,' he said. 'Faces and sexes are non-belly. For observing the breakdown of scholarship, nothing is better than an open belly. For diagnosis, on the other hand, you must know how to hold your instrument, combine modesty with audacity, palpate the obstacles. Since it's easy to confuse shitty viscera with the strong, odorous roots that help us meet life's great challenges, before the first cut it's best to get a whiff of the stiff below the midriff.'"

As he speaks, the doctor dissects, scrapes, flicks around in the flesh, raising any and all tissue as a question. The light is bright. The salt air parches the spectators' lips. Their shadows move constantly above the shark, which looks like a bat-angel with its skin held out by a nail on either side of its body.

"When I was a child I wanted to be a doctor some day. I thought I could contribute to science by finding out where babies come from. One day I heard my mother tell my father she was expecting. Expecting what? Five months later she said, 'It's moving,' the way you'd say it's raining or it's snowing. Her belly got bigger and bigger. Her legs swelled. She would go to see the doctor and come back saying, 'He examined me.' Ever since, the words see and examine have been entwined in my thinking, like the serpent symbols of my profession. My mother gave birth to triplets." So saying, he plunges a finger into the bloody mass of organs and pulls out the heart. "Triplets," he repeats, laughing fit to kill himself.

The amused and curious grins of the sailors change to grimaces of alarm. Discomfort, disgust. Faces close. Parched lips crack. Occident breathes noisily. Irène stands erect, arms wrapped about her chest like a straitjacket. Farther away, apart from the group, Derrick Tremblay leans on the rail and stares at the sea and the sun.

The doctor is inexhaustible. All the while he's talking Cybil is thinking, One can't act, talk and reflect all at the same time; this man belongs to another century. She is disturbed by the stream of words from the man and the flow of blood around the shark and along the hand cutting so knowledgeably, and can find no words to describe what she feels for Lemieux other than to call him a humanist, hesitating between the strong and the simpleminded senses of the term. Then they show up one by one, Jean-Paul Sartre's shifty eye, Georges Bataille's well-slicked grey hair, André Breton's Roman nose, Antonin Artaud's demented face, Michel Foucault's skull, yes, skull. Next she thinks that Thomas Lemieux is probably an unpretentious man like Doctor Aubon who used to care for her mother, and who, like so many others, had memorized what he had to to spend all day looking at teeth, bellies, cunts, vertebrae and corneas.

Thomas Lemieux seems to her real enough to deserve the title of fictional character. His arrogance, his angst, which Cybil associates with suffering greater than that of this one single pipe-sucking, bushy-browed individual, all qualifies him for a fictional role. Anyone who adapts his misery to a passion for life already has one foot in fiction. Anyone who can trace a path for thoughts and desires should live on.

On what grounds does one decide that a man deserves to enter the realm of fiction? Must one begin by imagining the child he once was (a little boy pedals with all his five years' worth of energy along a sidewalk mottled with winter's brown sand and calcium. He's talking to himself. Like a dotard or a simpleton. The words issue from his little pink mouth. He sows them to the four winds in the warmth of an early spring. He has known how to play with words for two years already. He knows you can put them in big suitcases and travel to the ends of the earth investigating those mysterious women called mommies) or robe him in such extreme sensitivity that a bagatelle will launch him beyond the purview of ordinary mortals? How are we to sculpt from each male's particularity the exemplary form of cliché in which each can recognize himself and fret his fill over the ambient morality?

Cybil turns to Irène for an answer as if Irène could help her understand the nature of a fictional character. Suddenly she knows one thing for certain: she must not make a character of Irène for Irène would then lose all her powers of life and creativity. Irène must stay alive, in the flesh, accessible.

As for Occident, Cybil no longer knows what to think. "Surrealistic," Jasmine said. Everything about her is so mysterious, yet paradoxically as open as those flat desert landscapes that lead to the shadowy routes of the cordilleras.

"The value that one attaches to a body," Lemieux continued, "is relative. Living or dead, a body is worth its weight in trade. Wars are terrible because bodies are left to rot whereas science needs them urgently. A dead body can be gathered up and sold for a price."

He removes the brain. "See, that's all there is. A ludicrous lump, electricity, a program. Add teeth and a few adjectives and compare with man. Depending how you use the adjectives, you either moralize or make up a yarn that will have people's eyes popping with terror. The only secrets man has are the ones he carries around inside him, tiny, child-size, grafted onto his enormous pretension."

The doctor wipes his forehead and sees his blood-stained hand. He intends to continue his monologue but his voice changes, becomes husky, to the point where he raises a hand over his head to signal that it's over and all should be cleared away. Sailors bustle about. Everything is committed to the sea. Occident moves away, flanked by the artists.

She suggests that her guests make the most of the light and the clear sky. "Tonight there's going to be a showing of pornographic movies. It's the custom. One halfway through the mission, another the night before returning to port. By tradition I attend the first. I'm asking you to do likewise out of solidarity. The *padre* is excused, it goes without saying. The showing will be in the library after dinner. You'll see it's not so awful. Rather elementary. Genitals. Close-ups. Heavy breathing. Flue-raking. Unless you consider heterosexuality as such unbearable, I assure you there will be nothing that could offend you. As for tomorrow and the days to come, you won't be bored. Pascal, Flash and Philippe will be your advisers."

PORNO

Cybil was seeing the library in artificial light for the first time. Four fluorescent tubes cast a harsh glare over thirty or so men sitting upright and patient on wobbly chairs. The card table had disappeared. A screen hid the porthole.

Cybil sits in the last row between Irène and Occident. Farther along, the captain and the doctor are exchanging a few words in low voices with an artificially blasé air.

The library is suddenly plunged in darkness. A warning in black and white: THIS FILM WAS PRODUCED BEFORE THE AIDS EPIDEMIC. YOU SHOULD ALWAYS APPLY A CONDOM BEFORE PENETRATION. Loud-laughingly, a Québécois sailor translates: "Kindly bag before penetration." Chair-scraping, coarse laughter, music, colours.

A postman is delivering mail in a suburban North American city. He passes local residents and greets them cheerily. He approaches a bungalow. Behind the house a woman sits by a swimming pool, leafing through a fashion magazine. The postman's face appears behind the wrought-iron fence blocking access to the garden. He holds up a parcel. The woman gets up and opens the gate. The postman takes a Bic from his pocket. The woman heads for the garden table on which to sign the customary form. She trips over a garden hose, falls in the water and splashes about with little screams of fright. The postman finally puts down his mailbag, leans down and holds out his hands to her. The woman's breasts overspill her bathing suit like two lifesaving buoys. She holds out her arms to the man. He helps her out of the water. She clings to him, dripping, quivering like a salmon trout. The man's suit is soaking wet. The woman apologizes. The man goes indoors. He takes off his shirt while the woman tries to dry him with a towel. With mutual apologies, the two come together. The man's hands go straight to the woman's huge, pink, dripping breasts. The man's hands massage the globes of flesh. The man's mouth sucks hungrily at her nipples. The woman's breasts and the man's tongue fill the screen. Fast forward. The woman pulls off the man's pants. She massages or polishes or dries the man's thighs, hard to say which. The man's member brushes the woman's cheek. The woman takes and licks the object as if to make it rounder, then pops it whole into her mouth between lips that never lose their brilliant redness. The object surfaces, then just as fast disappears again down the woman's throat. She is now gasping for breath. The woman's slender fingers and red-painted nails and the man's testicles fill the screen. The woman's face reappears, her mouth full of the man's member. She's distracted by a hair protruding from the corner of her mouth. She removes it. Fast forward. The woman is seen kneeling, ass on. The man pokes about, knowingly like a dog. Then there's a scramble of legs and coarse hairs and buttocks. The dick dips and dives in the woman's apparently aqueous sex. The sequence ends with an abundant flow of sperm which inundates all in its path from north to south.

The doorbell rings. A neighbour arrives wearing an Yves Saint-Laurent suit and green-frame glasses that make her look like a raccoon. She brings in a strawberry shortcake and compliments the mistress of the house on her negligee. Woman number one offers her a cup of tea. Woman number two looks at woman number one and runs her tongue over her lips. She keeps her mouth slightly open all the time like Isabelle Adjani playing Camille Claudel. She fingers the first woman's negligee, which she finally opens, exclaiming over the volume of the other's breasts. The two women look at each other. Woman number one slowly undoes the gold-tone buttons of the other's suit. The two size each other up in a big mirror, holding up their breasts like chic oblations. The man shows up at the end of the corridor.

Cybil wonders what the effect would be if the same scenes were in words. What would ass, vagina, penis, vulva and balls be like all crowded together? How might one picture the way *things* will go, plus their inevitable consequences once they've entered the language as imagination's relays? Would the words excite her? From the angle of enlarged sexes, who would be who, hyperfat in representation, with tongue and twat plugged into someone else?

While the man is being blown by woman number two, who then hands the bat to woman number one, who soon passes it to woman number two, Cybil beckons to Irène to follow her before the light comes on. Irène protests, says she's waiting for the end. Cybil decides to wait too.

The second movie begins. This time the story takes place at a seaside resort. Two couples are playing cards under an umbrella. Cybil observes the men's heads in front of her, which at the moment are motionless: one with hair combed smooth, one shaven, two bald, baseball and sailor caps, a ponytail. The books around the audience form a silent, inky mass. Here and there a white binding draws the eye. The library flickers with the soundtrack's repetitive waves. A men's adventure, this strange world of my solitude.

The show is over. Sounds of chairs being folded, coughing, lighters clicking alight. Smell of cigarettes. The men file out, each carrying his chair under his arm. Many are the knowing smiles amid the good nights and *buenas noches,* fireworks of artificial words and intonations.

Cybil takes Irène to her cabin with a crisp "Come on." The room is small, the bed littered with pages of her novel. Irène gathers them up one by one and puts them on the table then changes her mind and, putting on her glasses, asks if she can read some.

"I'm exhausted by simple things," Cybil replies, taking a bottle of port and two plastic glasses out of a drawer.

"Nothing is ever simple. A single metaphor and goodbye to naturalness. The slightest similarity between two objects of different but like nature provides exponentially increasing food for thought," Irène says in the tone of voice, the foreign accent that Cybil heard last autumn at the Dazibao Gallery. "Comparison stimulates ambition, envy, desire and, as I've said before, thinking that enables us to proceed to action, which is to say, to equalizing the differences between objects and individuals; or else increasing them to the point where there is no further ground for comparison. Life is a slipknot of useful comparisons and misleading metaphors, which accounts for our ability to shift the meanings of words to our advantage."

Apart from "nothing is ever simple," Cybil did not really understand what Irène was driving at. She poured the port. Isabelle Adjani's mouth opened like a stage curtain. Camille Claudel was breathing noisily in a slum dwelling somewhere in Paris under flood. The Seine formed a lake, of course, a mirror out of which beautiful trout kept leaping pink and silver, transforming the overcast sky into a sky of majestic dawn.

"In art," Irène said, "I mean in contemplation of a literary or pictorial work, it's always very tempting to draw a comparison with reality, which is to say, to reassign the enigmatic import of the work in our own conception of reality."

"Yes," Cybil replied as she undressed.

THE BROTHERS DEMERS

They came from Matane. So grandiose had the light of the sea appeared very early in their lives that each had lived in its aura expecting to arrive one day at an understanding of its mysteries.

The day their father was buried, they got drunk in a nude dancers bar. Thereupon, each had decided to leave. Pascal went to study computer programming at Laval University in Quebec City. Robert alias Flash headed for Montreal where, after working at Radio Shack for six months and Crazy Irving's for two years, he opened his own camera and computer store. Philippe signed on as a sailor aboard the Vancouver Oceanographic Institute research ship. In Quebec City, Pascal met a young woman from Martinique and in short order married her. As the years passed, the brothers fell into the habit of meeting in the Caribbean where they learned to be skilled divers and became enamoured of the blue that washes all human misery from one's eyes.

Their mother died ten years later. After the encoffinment and debauch, the *De Profundis* and the cemetery, the brothers lingered at length in a vacant lot, happy to be together again. With tears in their eyes, jaws set and hair blowing in the wind, they agreed to pool their knowledge and propose to the Maurice Lamontagne Institute the creation of a virtual reality program to simulate various methods of undersea diving. After three years of negotiations, they obtained the go-ahead to realize the project.

For the first working session with the artists, the Demers brothers had conceived of a freewheeling conversation during which each would tell his or her own story, the purpose being to create a climate of confidence.

On deck, divers and artists are sitting in a circle on wooden crates. Pascal's hefty calves, Flash's "cool" espadrilles, Philippe's runners, Cybil's sandals and Irène's bare feet form guidemarks on the deck surface, the clear blue of the sky on the shoulders of each participant. A short distance beyond, sailors are busy with movements common to housewives before the advent of electricity.

PHILIPPE

At first everything is blue. Dizzyingly blue. One's eyes adapt gradually, but they remain profoundly marked by that first fascination. The body, you'll see that the body – it's as if the body reorganized one's thoughts so they overlap in a natural way. The body becomes pure sensation, with close-ups of well-being coming by like schools of magical fish. No point thinking about the abyss. It simply enters us, a sum of emotions impossible to enumerate. What's important is the depth. Descending.

PASCAL

I think it would be good first of all to recall the names of devices that have helped us steadily go a little deeper all the time: the tuba, inflated goatskin, mask, air cylinder, hard-hat diving suit; the submersible lamp, cage, diving bell, bathysphere, bathyscaphe, diving saucers like *Denise,* and the wonder of wonders, the *Nautilus.* Without treasure hunting and the urge to break records, we'd still know mighty little about the bowels of the fabulous abyss the ocean used to be.

FLASH

To see, to see more and better all the time. Without motion-picture cameras and screens, we'd be like those word-nuts who think their own senses should be proof enough of underwater life. They come out of the water and dive straight into writing their memoirs. You can't trust that handful of men who've spent their lives hiding under the skirts of the sea. The sea can be beautiful, I'll agree, but it's well proven that all those who've looked at reality from below have coloured it by burying it under tons of metaphors which only bolster the superstitions we've been up against since Noah. I'd far rather trust the eight hundred frames that each of the *Nautilus*'s cameras can produce on each descent into the bathypelagic night.

PHILIPPE

Fear, Flash, you're forgetting fear, that feeling of suffocating, that desperate need to count your fingers to make sure you won't sink into narcosis. Fear, Flash, how can you forget fear's not just an image, it'll never be just an image, this thing that's one's own unquiet body surrounded by all that immensity.

PASCAL

Papa always said a man must never be afraid but must live as if he's under constant threat, so he'll learn to control himself. Whatever you do you must keep from crying out like a man who's afraid.

FLASH

Why get wet when we can acquire knowledge at a distance, make the most inaccessible worlds ours, learn how to do difficult jobs without paying the price in fear for our bodies? You artists don't know how lucky you are to be working with us.

PASCAL

Careful now. We mustn't mix apples and oranges. Forgive us, when we talk we sometimes confuse the strong feelings we get straight from the sea with what our eyes have seen behind the camera and what we feel in virtual settings. Sometimes there's reason to worry over this confusion, but since you've never been down there you'll be running no risk. The accessories are relatively easy to handle, as you'll see. It won't be long before you're comfortable with the Dynamic Wrist, the Dexterous HandMaster and the joystick.

IRÈNE

You really think so?

PHILIPPE

Your capacity for wonder will be the important thing.

FLASH

The more you give yourself to playing with your identity, the more and stronger the sensations you'll have. *You become what you feel* increasingly as the dive proceeds.

PHILIPPE

The strongest feelings I ever had, I had in my mother's bedroom.

PASCAL

Yes! Just imagine, Philippe has written a program that lets us inside our mother's bedroom! The way she'd fixed it up after Papa died. We use it all the time. It's like a little sanctuary for us. We go in and, depending how we've programmed it, Maman is sleeping or putting on her makeup or changing her dress or looking out the window. We can kiss her, sit on the edge of her bed and take her hand, draw the curtains, dust the pictures and knickknacks, help her with the zipper on her dress or a piece of jewellery, bring her a cup of tea. It's very moving, you know.

PHILIPPE

Each time I go into Maman's room, the present equals memory.

PASCAL

The feature that lets you touch and be touched is called "dataglove." In French we sometimes say *main symbolique*. This is one of the things that for five days is going to let you sweep your way through schools of fish so dense they're like curtains, stroke dolphins, touch and feel the most outlandish forms of life in the dimmest imaginable light. Virtual touch stimulates the imagination. In my case, it gives me the energy of ten.

FLASH

The visiohelmet is the primary source of information for moving about in a virtual environment. Our model gives a range of vision of 50 degrees on the horizontal axis and 70 on the vertical.

PHILIPPE

Don't bother your heads with all those details. What's important is to love being there. To have the first dive banish all thought of death forever.

The sun beats down. Heady feelings. Pascal pronounces the word depth. The double-time sensation catches up with Cybil.

"Depth" resonates, hits she's not sure what, the way you touch bottom with the oars when approaching shore. The word wobbles its single syllable in the stifling air, oscillates horizontally as on a television screen, then stabilizes at the surface of meanings, radiates in depth. Depth is a word but is already turning into a space: a hotel room with a queen-size bed, two bedside tables, a chair, an easy chair, a dressing table and a television set. The window looks onto a fire escape. The curtains are drawn and despite the poor lighting their shell motif is readily discernible. Cybil enters the room, lays the key on a bedside table. Such a present feeling.

reality *VIRTUALREALITY*VIRTUALREALITY*virtual*reality *VIRTUAL*r

eality *VIRTUALREALITY*VIRTUALREALITY*virtual*reality *VIRTUAL*re

Reality superimposed itself on reality. There was something heady indeed about the blue, something beguiling, begging to be crossed through. Corals sprang to view, like exploded rose petals to be touched gently. I learned to float with aplomb and with the current, and to resist it hand and foot in order to steer around large lustrous obstacles. Fascinated to have these arabesques assure my equilibrium in the lavish blue, I swam serenely toward the bottom, borne by a state of euphoria the like of which I had never felt before that day. Fluidity of gesture. A current of happiness and my skin breathing straight from the water's caress. Very soon I found myself in a forest of kelp, curious and intrigued at first, then careful to avoid the wrack fronds that could wrap around me like an inescapable trap.

No notion whatever of time. Nothing but a space open to impressions. Being, living tissue gobbled up by the unknown. A vacillation of senses amid new meanings, channelling energy through one's blood vessels toward new sources of energy.

In exemplary solitude, a slow, horizontal me in a watery dream that added to the wonder of dreaming.

Water that had swallowed the tears and bodies of thousands of women drowned, this same water in its unreal depth allowed me to be like a sponge. I soaked up the sweat and tears, all the liquids deposited deep in the abyss by the dangerous thinking that had compelled so many women to hurl themselves into it alive or become caught and dragged down, discouraged that terra firma had failed utterly to fulfil its promise of life.

I was out of context, close to meaning and at the same time removed from things that ravage the senses. I was a floating, animal, fabulous thing brimming with good will.

I wanted to observe everything. Yet no way could I hold my attention longer than a second on a single creature or a single coral. Either the object would become part of my silence and acquire such proportions that I would let the substance bearing its stories and anecdotes go to my head, or it would slip away, leaving me alone in the midst of an explosion of visual fragments that I could clearly not manage to visualize or contextualize.

Suddenly I was thirsty. An immeasurable thirst that grew as my eye synthesized the present.

I was present and nothing but, an illusion of perfect present, devoid of story or any attachment. Locked in a present which all my life I had proclaimed essential for doing justice to the intelligence of our senses. Now there was too much present. I tore off the visiohelmet and gloves, exhausted and trembling.

Philippe handed me a glass of water. Beside me, Irène was making little hand gestures. I could see her chin and cheeks moving constantly, animated by all that rich, eventful life played out in the screens that her eyes had become.

That evening, although I was tired, I fell upon my manuscript as if it held a solution capable of foiling the double time. As if entering fiction were the only way to return to reality. A strange thing happened: the sentences, instead of following sequentially and obediently one after the other, superimposed themselves one over the other, worrisome and transparent like a desire to surf on words, eliminating risk of harm by meaning. Obedience on the one hand, superficiality on the other. Meaning checkmated. The present was never-ending.

A world was dramatizing in me. Characters were filling the universe with their superiority as talking beings. I wanted to rework the dialogue begun between La Sixtine and Cybil Noland, but there was already too much body between them. I thought briefly that I would have to take a place myself between them. Take the place of one, put myself in the place of the other, as philosophers do sometimes the better to *seem* as well as *be* at this century's end, when, moving from posture to posture as others move from city to city, they smear themselves with another's scent and go about giving it off, taking care afterwards to moisten their lips with a vigorous sweep of the tongue.

Sleep came.

And a dream. I'm walking on René-Lévesque Boulevard under an adequate sky. Outside Mary Queen of the World Cathedral, tour buses, grey mastodons. On the cathedral steps, emaciated men hold out baseball caps for charity as others do their hands. I go in. I walk up the main aisle. Large pictures on either side draw my attention. Long-haired Indians, French soldiers, women named Jeanne Mance, Marguerite Bourgeois, Mère d'Youville. A hospital burns, Indians paddle. Their canoe is in imminent risk of being swept away by the raging waters. A painting in the left arcade of the transept intrigues me. I approach. A title: *The Martyrdom of the Jesuit Fathers J. de Brébeuf and G. Lalemant in the Land of the Hurons 1649*. Indians are sitting around a wood fire. In the middle, I recognize *Padre* Sinocchio. Bare-chested, hands bound to a wooden stake, he is beseeching heaven. Around his neck, a necklace of red-hot polished stones cut in the shape of tomahawks. In the background, another Jesuit is victim of the laws of perspective. Their faces show no trace of pain, hatred or cruelty. Sinocchio is intent, his gaze turned patiently toward Heaven. The Indians have the peaceful and peaceable look of people basking in the first days of spring. I swim my way out by the door opposite the Queen Elizabeth Hotel. There I climb into a calèche without histrionics. At the front a narrow metal cylinder containing a whip and a small Quebec flag. The driver smiles. "Every nation at least has a flag." We ride down to Old Montreal. The driver announces Pointe-à-Callières and talks about superimposed stratas, archeology, languages and cultures. In the harbour I notice a container ship named RIMOUSKI. The city horse trots along among the cars and trucks. At a red light, it turns into a mythical animal, a fugitive from faraway caves. Again it changes, trotting now through Sherwood Forest, cannons, fetlocks and coronets sweeping the high grass along the path, then makes like a sleepy sumpter standing in a field of millet. A tartar gallops hell-bent across a desert plain. Amazon, you're dreaming.

∾

The first thing next morning, I went looking for Occident to confide my worries over the book. Over the book and the future. I ended up on deck unsuccessful. A little gust of wind on my cheeks. Such beauty, such pleasure in the beauty of the day and the sea. Fifteen metres away, Thomas Lemieux was standing straight, gazing into the luminous distance of the morning. He was drumming on the rail, his forefingers tapping, an orgy of tap-taps borne by the wind in my direction. Face turned to the sun, eyelids closed, mouth round and filled with mimicry and contortion, his voice would whisper then swell like a rock-singer's, barking yesses and nos, *yes, vibrato* of fingertaps, melody. *Beat.* Silence. He would slowly drink in the wind and hold still until with tap and ratata and little jerks of hips, the sounds would spew anew from far down a ruined throat: *"If you see the wonder . . . I have a dream . . . I believe in angels."*[12]

As though he had breathed my presence, Lemieux turned toward me just as I was preparing to turn and retrace my steps, embarrassed to see him thus or so caught up in the beauty of the day. Our eyes met. A character.

Flash was looking for me. With virile flourish, he consulted his watch. "Let's hurry. Strong sensations today." Minutes later, hooked up and masked, I was diving in a new world. A gloomy landscape. Tall, chimney-shaped rocks spewing black, very black water. At the base of the chimney, a colony of red worms rooted inside large white tubes. All around, white fish, brachyuran crabs, clams, small octopuses. I look, incredulous and wary. Tremors. Falling rubble. A feeling of being swept away like a grain of sand, a puny speck of dust amid mighty forces. I don't know what it is I'm seeing, am unable to imagine what I'm seeing. I repeat the several words pronounced by Flash before the session: *gja* of great depth, black smoke-holes, white diffusers. *Zoarcidae, Serpulidae.* Now I skirt a dusky wall, a wall of dangerous silence, solid as slickensides. I skirt a wall of silence. Everything in me trembles.

❧

At dinner, the feeling of double time was devastating. As though by collusion among us, we were all dressed in black except Occident, who was wearing a turquoise jacket and whose eyes that night betrayed unparalleled melancholy.

For several days, Irène had ceased to take part in the conversation, keeping her visualizer's orality for the lyrico-techno-numerical affinities she shared with Flash. Occident was interrupting the men less and less often. For my own part, I was locked in a silence which, the further I sank into it, the more surely ruined all hope of sociability in me. Thomas Lemieux did not like our silence. He saw in it a plot, reproach, rejection, I don't know which. With each sentence, he hinted at doors left ajar. For us. He was extending his hand, constantly a line. And so he had barely finished his soup this evening before throwing out, like a pair of dice in the middle of the table: "Morality, let's talk about the morality of women." Five seconds, ten seconds went by. Lemieux was watching for the slightest change in our faces. A sigh or frown would have reassured him. Labour lost. Irène fiddled with her left earring. I kept studying the colour of the wine in my glass. Occident was trying to catch her breath. Lemieux looked at us, one after the other. Thoroughly disappointed, he said finally, "But. Today. Since morality divides into as many individuals as it takes for society to turn a profit, since a moralist is a busy lobbyist, since we launder evil the way the Mafia launders its money, since morality is a respectable and media-wise currency, is it still possible to be up in arms elsewhere than within one's own four walls?" To dream, be indignant collectively. He was right. Nobody did it any more. There were fads, certainly, causes that people rallied to out of curiosity. The gregarious instinct was still intact. Each followed individually. But no crowd reaction, true enough.

I must have looked pensive. Not knowing whether he had touched a nerve, Lemieux spoke directly to me. "Yes, I know, Cybil, you take me for a crank. A doctor has a soft time of it, a broad back too. He took a vow not to close his eyes to pain; his knowledge of the body, man and death is a lucrative investment. I know all your little writer's clichés."

He composed himself. "Nevertheless, it's a simple question. I'm asking you if you think women can still be collectively indignant over their misfortune." Misfortune, he had said misfortune as if it were a matter of chance, a piece of bad luck. He continued, now making himself positively odious. "Should we make a connection between women's morality and the 'business' of hope?" He glared at us, ignoring Carlos Loïc Nadeau's expression of annoyance and *Padre* Sinocchio's fit of agitation. "Business of hope" was his term for the recent phenomenon wherein a person, usually a woman, stricken by, say, the violent death of a daughter, must rebuild a life through petitions, press conferences and public soul-baring. "Mind you," he continued, "all that is explainable since without collective anger it's each for oneself with one's lawyers and the media, for whom personal disaster tastes of profit. Yes, ladies, you have won: private lives are henceforth the stuff of politics."

❧

When I went back to my cabin that night, I was overcome by an irresistible desire for details. A hidden disorder ruled my thoughts, forcing me to alternate reality, a dream state, and the other, so-called virtual reality which from now on was part of each one's perception of reality. I had begun to dream again as I had the previous year after receiving Occident's early letters. States of mind, of dream, lucidity and laissez-bellyache followed one after another at a rate that demanded its own luxuriance of details and recurrent motifs. Too much information. Too much feeling. Here, I suppressed reality for the benefit of fiction. There, at the far side of a dream state, I restored reality. Elsewhere, I had eyes only for elsewhere, wherein all could be recomposed figuratively. Not one moment of respite. Thousands of images offered themselves, virtual liaisons between the world and an increasingly uneasy me, a me hurtling on in obedience to I know not what insatiable need to grasp everything.

I reread my manuscript. I redefined the buildings in the armed city, which soon had the earmarks of a fantasy city. I described at length the reflection of palm trees in the bumpers of limousines and in the tinted spectacles of passersby. I added details to a point where they cast a wan, grey light of day in which I found myself sitting on the damp grass in a big park with a book in my hand.

Hyde Park. People are making traffic around me. A pants cuff, the muscular calves of a woman jogging, a child on a tricycle. Since I'm reading, I underline a word or sentence now and then. Cumberland Gate, a woman dressed in a red slicker marches resolutely toward Speaker's Corner, disappears from my field of vision, reappears, a small suitcase in her hand. She walks proudly, almost straight for me, one might say. She stops, puts her suitcase down, opens it and takes out a small wooden stool which she unfolds with a resounding snap. Immediately, three tourists gather round, curious to hear her begin speaking.

"My life is all about life. Language is alive in my throat. Can you hear the vibration? My voice has been severely damaged by a dream. I used to dream among dreamers. The dreamers have left. I am now left by myself to listen to my broken voice. Every day, I wake up early to hear the sound of the city. 'Dear, dear! How queer everything is today! And yesterday things went on just as usual. I wonder if I've changed in the night? Let me think: was I the same when I got up this morning? I almost think I can remember feeling a little different. But if I'm not the same, the next question is, Who in the world am I? Ah, that's the great puzzle!'" [13]

The woman folds her stool and puts it back in the suitcase. The red slicker walks in my direction. She notices Victor Hugo's *Les travailleurs de la mer* lying on the grass. Our eyes meet. She leaps at the opportunity.

"My mother was French, you know, my father English. Every day he used to read his Anglo-Saxon *philofficers* whom my mother kept denigrating, holding up the genius of her own thinking ancestors in comparison. Revolted at the thought that women could forever be relegated to ignorance and insignificance, my father took to choosing the books I read. When I was fifteen he made me read *Essays on Truth and Idea* as if wishing to thrust me into the arms of the Absolute or have me forevermore wedged between *What* and *That*. I understood none of it, of course. The more so since at this time French and English words were beginning to sow terrible confusion in me. Slave, pain, habit, bite, pour, sale, poise, rot – every day the list grew longer – bride, feu, fine, plumet, roman, chat, femme, fond, mine, chair. Helpless halfway between English and French, I believed I was forevermore marooned in ambivalence. Then, with the years, words took flight and I became a dreamer. What about you? Do you dream?" she said as she backed away with the rain trickling down her slicker in little grey runnels, and added, "*'However, she soon made out that she was in the pool of tears which she had wept when she was nine feet high.'*"[14]

⌒

The image of the Hyde Park woman persisted. I awoke chewing over those words by Lewis Carroll. Rain was drumming on the glass of the porthole. It was going to be a beastly day. I was becoming increasingly discouraged. Never would I be able to weave the bridge between Irène and me that was essential if Occident's book was to see the light of day. Each of us was digging herself deeper in her own world as if we were of different species, both specialized in the extreme. We were on assignment. It was going to take much more than the idea of a collaboration to enable us to portray the sea in its original flavour. There was too much solitude on this boat. Too many shibboleths, too much talk of discipline, not enough about the sea, not enough of that rare yen for eternity in our eyes. I was beginning to miss Montreal. Perhaps I was not a water woman after all.

⌒

I joined Irène and the Demers brothers. Pascal was calculating and Flash waxing impatient at everything. Philippe was being most attentive and respectful to his artists.

I settled into my "range of vision" only to be assailed by images, each more revolting than the last. Life. Life in all its forms of reproduction. A succession of close-ups intermingling eggs, larvae, fins, sperm flows, embryos, buccal shelter, peduncles, polyps. Asexual creatures – "Plankton," Pascal said, "means literally 'that which is born to wander'" – and others, sexual, strutted and embraced, viscous, red and obscene, gelatinous blobs caught up in genetic frenzy. In monsters big and small, LIFE bubbled over. Feed, prance, prey and puff up with pride. Come let me bugger you in the nexus of the plexus. Enough to raise one's *taedium vitae* à la Cioran or whoever. Viscous life in the living. Morula, blastula. Live creatures raising sea-floor ooze with a flip of the tail as they fell. It was not a pretty sight. Spectacular, though, these thousands of organs warding off the shades with their genders well in order.

The day was long. Full of disagreements over manoeuvres. After the evening meal, I went up to walk on deck. Sky of ink, total night. I went down to the library. Switched on the light. The fluorescent tubes flickered like cities at twilight. Soon a harsh light bathed the bookshelves and table. A smell of dust. It seemed to me as though thousands of years had passed since last week, as though time, having caused our hearts to beat and found a use for our thinking nature, had buried its pirouette and shadow here amid the paper. Occident had perhaps been right to make us examine our intentions in this place, because throughout our five days here, reaching now for a book, now for an illustration, Irène and I had felt mightily drawn to elsewhere; a taste for the future in us, amplified by being aware we were not yet there. From the few moments of intimacy shared with Irène, there remained the beginnings of a curious well-being, a sharing of the time when we had come close to being close. Now, we must compose with the troubling present of the *Symbol*.

Someone had left an issue of *Penthouse* lying on the table. I leafed through it. Women beside swimming pools. Women beside the sea. Women taking showers. Women wet and offered. I dozed off, my hand on the thigh of one of them.

Around me, women move about, heads turbaned in a towel, a towel about the waist, also naked or in bathing suits, some in underwear. Now and then my eye falls on buttocks, a pair of breasts or a pubis. I'm in the women's dressing room at a sports club. In the hall of mirrors, women dry their hair, others meticulously coat their bodies with scented creams that give their skin that sought-after satin glow. Some apply deodorants under their arms, others clean their ears with the air of one deeply pondering existence. Beauty spots, weals, scars, pimples. Old women with low-slung bellies, young lionesses in their thirties and others even younger and unformed. Bellys *fanci*nate me. These women carry a belly like a centre of gravity. Some proudly like a project, others like an obstacle impeding their gait. Scars are numerous: a stroke across, one horizontal, others cut diagonally, three centimetres, nine centimetres. Occident appears. To each woman she assigns an activity. Some will go and exercise at the pool; others, off to the sauna, will take care not to faint. Those sent to the whirlpool bath will be expected to write lists of the best subjects of conversation. Occident asks still others to clean the mirrors, making small circles with a soft rag. While cleaning, they will avoid looking at themselves in the mirrors. A bell rings. A bevy of little girls run in. Some wear first-communion dresses, others overalls or plaid skirts. They disperse, play tag, open the lockers, take out dresses, blouses and shoes that the women have carefully put away. Laughing, they parade with them. Leave fingermarks on the mirrors. The cleaners push them gently away but the children are so many that the mirrors are soon covered with the marks of their hands and halos left by their warm breath. Occident reappears. The little girls are frightened to see the woman with the scarred face smiling at them. Among them is a child wearing a centurion's breastplate, who films the scene. Occident compliments her and tells her that a mother, girl and little girl all have the same body; only their eyes are different, which is why they must protect their eyes above all.

◇

Pascal and Flash are absent. Philippe is waiting for us, a roguish air about him. He talks in circles. Finally he comes to the point. "On condition it stays between us, if you like I can let you into Maman's room." He is encouraged by our surprise and then enthusiasm. He boots. I throw a glance at Irène. She seems moved and touches my hand the way she did in the car in Rimouski.

The room is as big as an American hotel room. Pink and lilac. You can see the river from the window. A big bed. A bedside table on which a diary has been left. A dressing table. Standing profiled against the window – the mother. The woman is dressed in black silk pyjamas which at first sight could easily be taken for a tuxedo. My hand has moved. I can now get a close-up of the river, come close enough to see just its broad velvety back at low tide, or watch it sparkle from afar. I have a look around the room. On the bedside table, *Le Soleil* of November 27, 1943. The mother has moved from the window to the dressing table. She takes a Larousse dictionary from the top drawer. She turns the pages and stops at the word woman. She reads laboriously, following with her forefinger. Her mouth is full of whispers and murmurings as if she's making sure the words get from her eye to her mouth, then to her heart. Something's wrong. She chews at her cheek, rubs her eyes, massages around them in little circles. In a twinkling her face has changed: deep black strokes darken her eyelids.

As if she has divined my presence, she points to a fine gold chain, lifts her hair and turns the nape of her neck to me. I fasten the chain about her neck. Her hair is soft and gently curly. Soft is a word pronounced with rounded lips.

She gets up and goes to the bed, where she lies down with her arms crossed over her chest. I sit on the edge of the bed. She turns on her side with both knees doubled up against her belly. I stroke her unwrinkled cheek. I take her hand and lace her bony fingers with mine. She returns to her first position. The veins of her neck are swollen like those of singers who have exercised their voices over years. She stretches her arms above her head, languorous, relieved, but soon is gasping for breath, spreads her legs and bends her knees so that each leg makes an inverted V in the light. Suddenly. *I become her.* A terrible pain low in my back, low in my belly. The feeling that something is tearing in me. I breathe. Noisily reaching deep in long sequences inhaling and exhaling. Then there's a child in the room. The child is playing with a die.

AN OCCIDENTAL NIGHT

It was to be the last night. The ship would dock at La Plata at dawn.

During the evening meal, the men had sung songs of their country. The captain was pleased with the mission. He had offered champagne all round. They had eaten crab, licking their fingers. Occident had had an asthma attack. Irène declared herself transformed by the voyage.

The sun would soon be setting. The men went to the library for the last pornography session. The women went up on deck.

Elbows on the railing, they sink into the beauty of the so-called twilight distance. The sun orchestrates a double present with the flames and oranges and ruby reds it generates.

CYBIL

What a strange story you've had us live, Occident. What a harebrained world you chose to embroil us in to fuel a project whose train and thread I seem to have lost. By your will, the sea will be more foreign and less accessible to us than before we left. You have surrounded us with men and books and made us work behind a mask, our bodies wired. You pretended you would put us in touch with reality only to thrust us into a world of artifice.

OCCIDENT

There's a light breeze tonight but, mind, we don't speak lightly of light breezes. On the Beaufort scale there's a difference between a light breeze, gentle breeze, moderate breeze, fresh breeze and strong breeze. When the sea is calm it's said to be like a mirror. A breeze raises ripples, wavelets, foam, whitehorses and spray. Beyond this, we must use the terms gale, high wave, spindrift and breaking wave. From force ten on, you're in danger. At force twelve, the sea is entirely white. I haven't changed my mind, Cybil; a book should instruct us.

The sun is now lying flat on the sea. It cuts small notches fishbone-fashion in red ink on the sea's back.

CYBIL

Your ways are offensive, Occident. I was free to refuse your proposal, you will say. I was not, for you had seeded *elsewhere* in me like a dream.

OCCIDENT

I didn't disappoint you, then. If dreaming means being there without being there, you must agree that I made you dream beyond anything you ever hoped for. You accuse me unfairly. It's not in my power to free the dark forces holding you on shore. I have never questioned your freedom of expression. Don't blame me for your frustrations. An artist must be able to turn everything to account, including the deadwood that hinders the coming of thoughts.

Nothing remains on the horizon now but a slim line of colour, and soon it too is swallowed by the black. A felt-marker black capable of blotting out everything, crowding the earlier splendour into oblivion. A sailor comes on deck to announce that the library has been put back in order.

With its wall-like verticality, the night makes eyes ineffectual. Cybil has never known such a night. Nowhere in the world has the density of night seemed to press so cruelly around her. Nowhere has the vast world peopled with hopes and resentments been reduced to such pointlessness, such silence, a major obstacle to her understanding. A solid block of darkness. Heart beating at slow. A solitary heart immobilized like a life abstract in the heart of darkness. A walled night. Cultural closure. Too much of everything, a misleading metaphor mooching round in the silence. Too night. Only Occident's dry cough abrades the black mass of the night. Darkroom.

Now a clear, triumphal voice is heard. The voice wafts from far away. A suspiration. Who is who, this massive shadow in the night, who is there, moving Cybil with her breath?

VOICE

You will write this book in the midst of night, mingling your shadow with the shades, uniting the dead with the living, and all the necessary words with your overabundance of desire. You will refuse to choose from among this voice, the night and the sea, and will anoint yourself with their perfumes and immensity which awaken the body amid abundant declarations of undying love. In this language that was given to you, you will awaken dream monsters and legends and timepieces, all the truth of reality incrusted like the dust of time between the wings of angels and on carved madonnas, between the eyes of gargoyles and among the acanthus leaves on the Sun Life's columns. You will seek out every one of these voices, the high and low whose tones you hear even now, the recitative, the modulated strains of anxiety and fear, the cries of joy and pleasure, the enigmatic whisperings, the amorous murmurs in the pale light of morning. La Sixtine's music as she holds her bow with hand folded like an *origami*. The voice of the red-haired woman toppling down the abyss of laughter, giving, giving from her heart and from her belly. Irène's voice arguing with herself in her darkroom. Your ear you will place to the mouths of loud-voiced, angry women, fearless of the crudity and gravity of their words. You will kiss Occident on her ugly pink scar, shuddering with her in the memory of the time. You will teeter above the abyss and the water, and live in your vertigo. With eyes clear and alert, mouth creased with song and declarations and solemn oaths, you will disentwine the tangled shadows of your characters although bound yourself in their shade.

Because one could die beyond force ten, the voice transforms to a gleaming shape like a body just emerged from water. The voice is a bird, a head of hair, seaweed, a lyre bird, a manatee; is heard again, this time a source of light, an immense mirror bowsed at deck-rail height. Reflected there, a picture of Mage, Noland and DesRives standing close together as in the days when it was the fashion to represent the notion of a people by shoulder-to-shoulder characters. Occident in the middle, pale, one hand on Cybil's shoulder, the other resting on Irène's arm. Because of the mirror and its reverse image, the women are searching their picture beyond the reflection. The picture changes. The mirror becomes a screen. In extreme slow motion, generations of women rotate, showing their shoulders and profiles, their milk-filled breasts, their full warrior hips, their heads haloed or adorned with fruits, a lyre, a comb or the whole earth. Other, younger women wear schoolgirl berets among still others who are bareheaded with persistent, insistent eyes.

OCCIDENT

Only a few years ago, we could safely say that the sea was a continuing presence, an eternal new beginning. Now the future figures in its destiny. The future is our present. I came to want this book, a collaboration between you two, because I am haunted by the idea that the sea cannot much longer perform a symbol's role. I thought your art could pour balm on my fears, soothe the anguish of my foreboding. Is it not said that "abstraction eviscerates the symbol and makes a sign of it; that art, on the contrary, flees the sign and nourishes the symbol"?[15] Tell me, Irène, when does a symbol cease to be a symbol? Tell me, Cybil, when a word has lost its sense, does it founder, emptied forever of its mystery?

Irène seems to want to reply with one of those long pronouncements that turn her into an oracle of urban modernity, but she has barely taken off before the pronouncement folds like a stricken bull.

IRÈNE

How is it that you have so little to say about yourself?

OCCIDENT

I knew my mother only through paintings and photographs. Old pictures, prints, snapshots, drawings that my father surrounded himself with. I don't know what bonding with one's mother means. This has always seemed to me to justify a certain reserve regarding so-called private things. I excel at understanding and discoursing about anything not explainable by emotional or sentimental bonds. At this very moment, for instance, I'm shivering and trying to catch my breath, but don't ask me to explain it by anything other than my asthma and the light breeze that's blowing. All I know has come to me from books and the sensations accumulated in my nervous system over the years. My learning is bookish and my knowledge of the world purely physical. I do occasionally have shivers that might be related to some emotion or other, but since I don't cultivate intimate relationships, they simply do not matter to me. I have no trouble believing anything people tell me about themselves, on the other hand. But beyond my understanding of the biological and chemical laws that have us react against any form of aggression, I'm emotionally illiterate. I have no idea how to interpret motivations or good or evil intentions. For instance, I've known Carlos Loïc Nadeau for years. He has told me his life story, indicated his tastes, expressed his political convictions a hundred times. Each time, I have believed everything he was saying. Yet I'm powerless to understand his temper tantrums, his sudden swings of mood, his determination to win at all cost when we have differences of opinion on, say, the risks of certain core-sampling manoeuvres.

IRÈNE

But you grew up somewhere!

OCCIDENT

I spent part of my childhood by the Mediterranean, the other part between the coasts of France and England. The truth is, I grew up in the casinos owned by my father. Where the losers always outnumber the winners. I lived where hiding what one is up to, bluffing and cultivating a poker face are common currency. This is the first time I've ever told this story. Though it's not a story properly speaking. Just a bit of red and black, and a big green mat where the chips accumulate, to be raked in mechanically by the long arms of the dealers. Décor. The usual. Seats open, empty, occupied. Men ruined, women consumed, bank notes, numbers. One verb alone counts: win.

At twenty, I bet everything I owned on the number 3. I won. I left for the west coast of the United States. I studied at the university at San Diego during the week, and on weekends I travelled to Las Vegas where I worked as a cashier. An oceanographer navigating the desert. Don't laugh. The Latin word *mare* comes from the sanskrit *maru* which means desert, you know. One day I was offered a job at Rimouski.

What a curious night! A little while ago, I thought I heard a siren's voice. Sirens appear in all kinds of weather. Poetry, you'll say, Cybil. Probably. In the Byzantine era it was customary among scholars to refer to each other mutually as "siren." On each of my voyages I've been told incredible stories, which I have believed of course. The Fijian siren. A monster built from scratch by a Japanese fisherman who sewed a salmon's tail to the upper body of an orangutan. She was bought by an American for six thousand dollars. Since the beginning of time there have been fine and terrible sirens – imaginary, cobbled from odds and ends, or real, palpable flesh. For my own part, they have always brought me good fortune, not only those that inhabit the sea but also those to be found in convents and manuscripts.

Wheezing, Occident leads the artists to three long wooden deck chairs which look in the darkness like recumbent funerary figures. The women are sitting now with feet up and eyes large, gazing at the starry night. A gentle breeze wafts across their bodies, caresses hair and sometimes the tips of breasts. Like a great green casino mat open for all bets, the immensity of the universe is once more present, brazenly offering itself for rapturous sighs. Each star is like a golden pen-point. Pens trace dotted lines suggesting dog, bear, horns and sails. Between constellations there are paths along which questions wend like languorous gliders. Irresistible questions whose sense is to be dissipated, turned to gold dust, to milky, soothing beauty.

Occident is coughing more and more. Whistling bronchial tubes. Spasms. Heaving chest. Gestures suddenly incoherent. Cybil and Irène stand up in alarm. The wind lashes at their legs.

Irène decides to go and find Thomas Lemieux.

Occident died at dawn. The doctor had arrived on deck at the run, followed by the captain and Derrick Tremblay. The three men had busied themselves around Occident after waving Cybil and Irène away as they would curious strangers. Then they had carried her to the library and laid her with utmost tenderness on the floor. *Padre* Sinocchio had arrived, pale and trembling. Cybil stayed near the porthole. The fluorescent tubes cast a pale, sinister light over the faces. Derrick Tremblay chewed at his lower lip. The captain asked Irène to go and fetch the video camera. Irène filmed. Everything spun. The men whispered. Extremely unctuous words issued from the *padre*'s mouth. The doctor kept passing his hand across Occident's forehead as if trying to wipe away any evil thoughts of death that might already have taken form in her head. At the roots, her hair was white.

She had turned up the palm of her left hand. It lay there, extended, appealing for another hand. Cybil understood. She threaded her way between the men to the side of this woman who, she was now convinced, had changed the horizon of her life. The blue eyes were roaming hither and yon, their sea-blue going abstract, who knows where. Cybil brought her face close to the head. The cheek, the skin, the scar had an odour now. The lips were close to moving, trying to speak, but the men would in no way yield their places beside the dying woman, and Cybil was politely but firmly returned to the background of the scene. And so Occident's last words went to nest in mystery in the ear of Thomas Lemieux.

At La Plata, Juan Existo was waiting on the wharf. The wives and fiancées jostled behind him, eager for reunion. Juan was brought on board. The men held a meeting, discussed, made decisions, prepared a press release. Took care of everything in minutest detail. Papers, documents, certificates.

Occident was cremated. Carlos Loïc Nadeau was to scatter her ashes on entering the Gulf of St. Lawrence.

Hotel Carrasco

I booked into the Hotel Carrasco. The one in the poster I had noticed during the stop at Montevideo. From my window I look out on the *río*, on the sea, I could say for that matter. I shall stay here as long as I need. I spend every day writing the text of the book Occident wanted so much. In the evening I go for walks in the streets of Carrasco, or on the promenade by the sea. The double-time feeling has gone. I have returned to being what I have always been: alone. There is no need to tell everything. I move about on ocean bottoms. I write about spines, monsters, mouths and tails.

Every morning, as at Rimouski, "the sea is the foliage of all the rivers."[16] Distinguished strollers on the promenade. An appalling sun. I revel in the heady blue. The hotel is immense. Turn-of-the-century splendour. Few guests. The ceilings are high. Magnificent columns, chandeliers. Mirrors that swallow the shadows as one passes, brief dismay on passing one's own likeness. Now and then I meet a group of filmmakers here to present their works at the Montevideo

Film Festival. The corridors are wide enough for them to walk four abreast without my having to stand aside for them. The dining room would be empty without them. And silent. There's a single woman in the group. A very old woman who, they say, knew Garbo, Dietrich and Riefenstahl. The filmmakers are very attentive to her. Age makes a woman respectable.

They told me at the desk that artists traditionally stay at this hotel, where it is easy to imagine and dream. The splendour of the past is not lost on anyone. The past attracts because, emptied of the bodies that once peopled the bustle of daily life, their humours and secretions functioning at full capacity, repopulating it with fleshly presences appeals to the imagination. And so, while regretting not having been there in person, we discover ourselves gradually bestowing faces and outlooks, feelings and behaviour on more recent beings who will see to it that we lack nothing while pondering our disappearance.

There is a casino in the hotel. I have yet to set foot in it.

I suspect I won't ever manage without Occident and Irène any more. Whatever happens, their voices will go with me, contemporary and wondrous, like arguments in favour of life in the sonorous world of change and fiction.

Some nights I feel Occident's presence with excruciating sharpness. Then, though it makes no sense, I call up La Sixtine's image. We sit on the edge of the bed with the severe expression desire sometimes gives. We get up and dance, entwined in the succession of hours. I don't know what will become of Cybil Noland the character. Before anything else, I must finish the text of this book of Occident's, out of respect for her. A great many words for my survival.

Impossible to forget that final scene. The proffered hand. Above all, the odour. I am ashamed. I should have pushed past the *padre,* the captain and the doctor to take my place beside her. So as to commune with her distress, her fear, to listen with such presence of mind that life would have won the day. There's no excuse for my passivity. I lost face and my honour not fighting for my place beside Occident.

Thomas Lemieux had not left with the ship and crew. He signed all the documents. After the cremation he announced that he would not set foot again on the *Symbol,* that he was going south to Patagonia, and then he invited us – the Demers brothers, Derrick Tremblay, Irène and me – to a restaurant in La Boca, where we drank to excess until dawn while making word plays on death. Such lighthearted slayings. Foolery which no doubt made us look like barbarians in the eyes of the *porteños.* Sorrow. Touching bottom. The next day the *Symbol* set sail northward. Irène flew off to Montreal and her screens. A character.

After being up all night at La Boca, I went back to the hotel. I slept for three hours. I went out again around noon, the hour when the sun is murderous. I spent the day wandering about Buenos Aires. I marched with the Mothers of the Plaza de Mayo. Around seven in the evening I returned to the hotel. I was handed a letter from Irène. Another from Lemieux. I reserved a plane ticket for Montevideo and a room at the Hotel Carrasco. I shall call the book *The Speed of Silence.* Or perhaps *Bellys.*

ONE SINGLE BODY
FOR COMPARISON

"There is another problem – how is one to judge an author's sincerity."

— ROGER CAILLOIS

We happen at times to smile without cause, I mean lightly, a fleeting grace passing through our eyes like a shadow in a shiver's duration at the always-heady thought of renaissance. Against the window, spattering rain like a school of fish, a small sudden undulation seen from the corner of one's eye in the momentarily darkened light.

They put me in a hotel in the heart of Old Montreal. From the seventeenth floor, Montreal, the Old Port, its sheds. A glimpse of the great river from the corner window. The publisher has sent flowers. Three lilies and a stem of orchid. The lilies' scent is pregnant. I've ordered up some tea. The sugar bowl looks like a volcano.

It's a relief to have this whole story behind me. Five years already. I spend part of my time with the translator and the publicist. We weave about through the geography and the present, broaching several subjects at once to make sure not to forget anything. We talk about time. We get away from it with short sentences. We plan the next day's schedule putting our heads together over steaming cups of black coffee. We advance hypotheses on the feelings that emerge after we've been tackling the text. I recount my first visit to Montreal, to Place Ville Marie which was then being built. Then a second, more recent trip when I was greatly pleased to discover a French city. I let the past flow. The young translator is interested in the present, overflows with the energy of the present. Says how happy she is that the French translation should be Québécoise.

The view from my room is unmatchable. The river breathes. In the distance, a tender green panoply, the green of apples and lusty love and tarragon, a young-season-flavoured green.

The publisher gave me a bound copy of the translation. I stroke the book's white binding. Sharkskin, curiously smooth like satin. Later that evening, surrounded by sober, pathetic people, I talked about the danger in trying to polish too much. Polishing one's text, one's words, one's life. The danger of dulling reality. There were people who talked about fashion in writing while others held to the generational phenomenon, insisting that certain eras rather than others facilitate the emergence of new voices. One woman said she couldn't tell the difference between the tiffs and ifs of an era.

Absurd, this idea that there are easy eras for writing. As if sense were not constantly to be revisited amid questions charged with myths and electricity. The innate understanding we have of death and beauty can only test our beliefs, sharpen our sensual appetites. No, there never have been easy eras. Science, violence and death are always contemporary, burning hoops that mesmerize the wild, spirited creatures we are, and inclined as we are to reject idle time and easy parts.

London seems far away. The world is changing. We must take advantage of change. Others before us have believed in this. It's been done. We know it's so. In our genes, we're promised so.

During interviews, I'm careful not to say *at the time.* There in midsentence, the impression *I don't write any more* would be too painful. Of course, these things do happen – burnout, boredom, defeat, the farcical phenomenon of laissez-bellyache. Occurring just like that, *I don't write any more* might tarnish the idea of fulfilment I'm determined to convey, the idea you get when you cultivate utopias in language as you would forget-me-nots. If some day it befell me not to write any more, I would demand reparation. Yes, I would take vengeance for that horrible sensation.

I'm often questioned about my mother's French origins, my double identity. People are curious about my almost-French French accent. They like me because of Virginia Woolf, Emily Brontë or Radclyffe Hall. Existing in the father's language worries some of them. They make me revisit the past. I put myself in *their* place in history. Every day I phago-cytize part of their reality and their literature. The world is changing. Speaking French stirs me emotionally. I tell small, engaging anecdotes. What they like is "the English novelist," as if the term were simply the stuff of fantasy, a feast of symbols in which the sea and its shore excite the imagination, in which woman and cliff form a mysterious couple subject to wind-blown narrative forces.

No city sounds reach the seventeenth floor. Vertical silence. Montreal captivates me from my skull to my toes, with a horizontal pause at shoulder height. I'm turning over a new leaf. Last night I slept naked with the air-conditioning on. Slept without either good dreams or bad. A woman asleep in the middle of a big hotel room. How many births, natural deaths and rapes occurred, how many waves pounded on the shores of the world while I slept? What happens at dawn from east to west, at every dawn from north to south when I'm away, and when women, as they do in movies, hold out lustful arms to the coming day? Each time my chest expands and I breathe, mouth open against a white-sheet background in the blackness of the room, how goes the morality of men armed with morals?

Succumbing to the temptation not to write any more would be unspeakably gutless. During yesterday's interview, "Occident" got away from me. I know well there's a connection between writing and the feeling of omnipresence the word brings me, for it often makes me feel I'm right. The word got away from me. I immediately surrounded it with images, each an oxidant of the marvel of sound. I could have stopped there at the oral bit but I ploughed ahead, associating the Occident with progress, navigation and the vulgarization of the individual and his rapid ascent to the top of the hierarchy of species.

The translator says, "Translating you has not been a bed of roses. Your descriptions of the *pietàs,* your way of slowing things in cemeteries, of surrounding bronze and marble with a holographic haze to heighten the impression of presence and strangeness. And the sudden illusion of power you give. Power to touch, caress perhaps. One might say there are surds in your words. Yet every time one suspects an absence, a void, the words turn into ripe fruits bursting with energy. Ah yes, you have caught me off guard at times."

Ah yes has stayed in my mind as an expression of joy, a kind of eagerness for the raw pleasure of life, for the pleasure of a goal in life. A yes that one would say came from the heart heading for an elsewise elsewhere. *Ah yes* on her lips brought me back a pleasure from days gone by. Like, at the time, a series of little capers low in the belly giving the world harmonious proportions, a cheerful manner that makes peace with life while demanding its due in words both gentle and muscular.

Some mornings it crosses my mind that there are tender places in the world the way there are here and there on the surface of the body, unequally distributed so as to stimulate the urge to explore with the joyful notion that merely by following people's contours one may land in zones propitious for knowledge.

For part of the morning I hung round Mary Queen of the World Cathedral. I couldn't resist the urge I had to see the Delfosse paintings again. I don't know why these pictures have so long remained so deeply graven in my traveller's memory. Or perhaps it was the whole cathedral that fascinated me then. That predilection for small-scale reproduction on a continent so vast.

It could be that those around us have something to do with the characters we create. It could be, after all, that we're able to reproduce a joie de vivre by introducing as decorative motifs our torments and the odd weak argument not too far off joy.

Journalists: "It's said that you spent an extended period in Buenos Aires and that you knew Piazzola. At the time, you granted an interview to *La Nation* in which you declared, 'Here, I exist.' You have published nothing for five years; can it be concluded that [inaudible]? It has been reported that during your last visit to Quebec you asked to meet the author of *L'Euguélionne*[17] and the novelist Victor-Lévy Beaulieu. Is it true that at the last Paris Book Fair you almost came to blows with Camille Paglia and that Bernard-Henri Lévy had to step in between you?"

Altogether fascinating, these ideas we believe to be eternal but which live barely as long as graffiti, an election or a headache. However, I rejoice that fiction can make them so well and truly viable that their existence can never more be doubted.

"Let's come back," the translator said, "to beauty. I don't think we can do without it. We so desperately want enchantment. And love equally as much, aware how tiny and fragile we are before the immensity of the universe. The biological law whose rule blinds us to too vivid a source of light impels us constantly toward one whose touch may reassure us. Thus persists our feeling that we can reach out and touch light."

Fine weather. On the terrace, two men are displaying positively funereal arrogance. A young photographer has joined us, her eyes sparkling. The publis*her* has just put her in charge of the DOUBLE MISE imprint. "Poets, philosophers, computer graphics designers, photographers, painters, *name them, I'll match them.*" As a noisy band, we celebrate. Then, as if she can't sit still, she hauls us off to the Musée d'art contemporain to see the Andres Serrano exhibition. Several back lanes to negotiate because, she claims, when you take these small arteries you exercise your eye, increasing its reflexive capacity. She says, "A lane is to the eye what a siren is to the ear – disturbing."

At the museum we look at death. Impeccable.

One single body to teach us about pleasure. One single body for presence and absence, and to cut the jagged shape of thoughts out of time. One single body to satisfy our craving for light and sea. One single body for finding the necessary words and obliging us to repeat them. The same one for comparing. A body of memory for inventing and progressing toward silence.

Montreal's lanes make me think of the time when I was stringing words together like beads. Never any loose ends. Description: solid, wall-to-wall, concrete reality. A sick tree, a cat, a street sign, I described it. A woman sitting on a bench, I showed her face, her red hands, swollen legs, clothes spilling out of a rumpled shopping bag; at her feet, cigarette butts and every kind of filth stuck to the sidewalk. In the time it took to look up and see the upper floors of a residential tower, I described clouds, balconies, urban vertigo. Yes, it was easy for me then. In a manner of speaking I *de*scribed in writing "with my eyes closed." Later I was presumptuous enough to think that what I was writing was giving meaning to my life. Then *I don't write any more* struck me down.

Yesterday, the translator and I read selections from the novel on the radio. Time and culture in transition in our voices. Hers, husky yet melodious. Mine clearer, frail it sounded to me. I enunciate what I read with remembrance of my writing days. The smell of mint tea, Cecil Court and its shop windows full of old books. My studio. On rainy days, all my books stacked in a corner like a Tower of Babel, the view of Hyde Park with its chameleon green, the Serpentine's patch of blue. Here, I am always this same present, private thing entrenched in the urban din, a singular shadow in the daylight in which contemporary passersby pass by. Time moving into language, kicking against the traces for love of travel and places. On the radio, we are two voices staged on waves. And this brings us together.

On the radio again today. We talk passionately in impersonals. Whoever. One. People. Riding the current of great aesthetic principles, disposed to doing right, wreaking a little havoc and finding ourselves an aim in life, we deal with no one gently. We answer all questions with other people's sounds in our earphones like an echo of yesterday's material, and eagerly and hopefully concoct proposals of our own. We keep a straight face come what may.

A feeling of living at the future's edge, my own legitimacy destabilized in the midst of all the artifice. Reduced to reaching for a redundant world through pictorial intermediaries. Each for oneself, pockets full of vibrations, old sorrows and photocopies, holding out one's own small-screen universe. Far away, we're still far away. I look at the river and the neon culture all around it like a freeway. Civilization on the massive edge of civilization. Sometimes we go to strange lengths indeed to hide our tears.

I tire after a while. Speaking French moves me indescribably. Yet I can hold my own in Maman's language. The translator, who is sharp as anything, not to say as a tack, has observed both the discomfort and the ease with which I compose. She therefore sometimes speaks to me in English when the going gets tough. I'm grateful to her for throwing me a line this way, but strangely I no longer know nor am where we're at all of a sudden. Two or three sentences in English suffice to have me joining incoherent things, spear-carrying extras and other useful syllables not within her purview. I can see in her eyes she has figured that in my father's language I'm a gambler and don't hesitate to cheat. In this here language of his, I know I can win while looking as if I'm following the rules. But not following them at all.

French was first my mother's mouth, round O's, pet names, clucking tongue, shrimp-coloured pacifiers, the crunch of bread breaking in her hand. Dimples below her peepers whenever she laughed. Her breath on my nose when she pronounced *truffe,* giving herself Lady Larousse airs. French was *azur, azalée* and *tous azimuts* in all directions. Daybreak all pink and the colours she claimed to see in sounds when she stood against the window of a morning, and making a great circle of life with her arms, dressed me up in kisses and exquisite words. French was the beach. Brighton. My sister Adeline carried off by the waves because of a French word my mother could not translate and never did manage to pronounce in English.

The publisher on the line. There has been a death in the family. She is leaving tonight in great haste for Rimouski. The publicist will take care of everything, of me. In the fluster, our words overlap. Then tranquillity. Rimouski is no longer an abstract point in the atlas I held on my lap all that time, dreaming of the St. Lawrence, its dimension such that having no point of comparison I must needs look to the horizon to feed my imagination. Death too visits Rimouski.

The translator insists that the birth of a character transforms the light of morning, incorporates it in the great whole of ludic creative energy. All of which can compare with the birth of a myth. She says a character is never just a visitor. Although free to abandon a character whenever one feels inclined, one who invents someone else knows the other will always be up there ahead.

On television, we have five minutes to talk about eternity, that's the theme, and about my book. We're on live. We pounce on eternity with nerves on edge. During commercial breaks, the producer cracks his finger joints. The publicist watches us from a corner. Now it's over, a lovely summer-nity, you might say.

The future is a constant rumour that poisons present energy and keeps us continually on our guard. The future is a suspicious object, a bundle of communications left at the foot of an information booth and observed by specialists who are preparing to disarm it. When the future comes, the diversity of others makes no difference; there's always this extraordinary capacity of ours for voyaging, the excitement of open spaces and random mingling. The future roots us in fiction.

In the course of my conversations with the translator, I observe that we have paused over the same passages. We have come up short where the words in fact were offering an opening. Thus when going for the other hand part of *on the other hand,* we have come to a standstill amid the choices to be made, looking for a follow-up that would not compromise the meaning of the story, the configuration of destinies. The translator insists that literature is only a matter of *on the other hand.* To follow up, we talk at length about travelling, then spend the rest of the day at a Nautilus on Park Avenue.

Among the equipment, one single body for comparison, our muscles oiled, tensed in the pure wonder of the fleshly present. A single skeleton for gauging the weight of a day, the lightness and strength of arms and legs. The body's elasticity, its electricity. Soon we're awash and ready to rest. After the shower, we avoid looking each other in the eye. The translator says, "In French, if you leave out *ou* and *où* and the auxiliaries, there are only seven words composed exclusively of vowels: two mammals, one bird, one sense, a toy, *oui,* which can be a noun or amount to an affirmative proposition, and *eau,* which has no smell or flavour like colours, but when produced in the mouth plays havoc with our imaginations."

When we separate a thought from a character, the thought lands at the far side of our intentions, does it not? We refer to a thought that has lost its character as a fragment. Volubility is something else. Rapid like a fragment but unreliable. Useful on the other hand for interrupting those more talkative than ourselves and for getting the normal out of our navels.

We're agreed: there are voids in language that are not from silence and in no way explain the second state in which a character sometimes lands. Lying in wait for vertigo and tension are voids that wound the character and restore the author's confidence.

The translator never ceases to surprise me. Impression that she devours too much of the present, too much of everything, fast with her red mouth lit up like a lighthearted device by day, a signal fire by night. A respectful connivance is developing between us. Beyond the difference in age and culture, there is a kind of truth binding us, demanding fabulation. Today, while crossing Lafontaine Park, we addressed each other as *tu*.

Later, well into the night, I thought it probably a mistake to hope that fiction might bring on some new kind of dream and bare the soul to the point of showing the body's frame in flutes of bone and reed. What we should be doing instead, I thought, was close in, get to the obscene part of fiction, unloose this thing that gets ahead of us, makes us want to play with fire, let it do its thing. We should be imagining fiction that, with our latter-day unintelligence about the present, brings us to the brink in language.

Notre Dame Street, Common Street. The past oozes from the walls of buildings: Southam Printing Company Montreal, Potato Distributors Ltd., the Standard Paper Box Co. Limited. The past graven in stone, Bank of Montreal, Molson Bank; the present in neon, coloured French. I buy the Saturday papers. Here a review of the novel. My picture. There an interview, with a picture of the author and the translator. The picture was taken at the Mount Royal lookout. Montreal in the background. As though looking in a direction dictated by the wind and intuition, we seem to be seeing afar.

I peer closely at my picture, comparing it with *at the time*. I'm smiling, gaiety's courage deep in my eyes as though the language experience has served to accentuate my features. One day a woman who loved me took five seconds to take three pictures of me with the sea as background. In the first I live and breathe, I am what I am. In the second I'm neck, chins and eyebrows with a peculiar slow smile. In the third I'm a stranger to myself in close-up. Out of alignment with the sea. I tore this one into little pieces. I've never forgotten the look on the face of the madwoman who tore me up.

The lilies have faded. I have come down to the florist's to buy some wildflowers. There's a shopping mall built on the old fortifications of the city next to the hotel. I walk past the shops. Behind a row of plants I discover a fountain, a liquid tomb endlessly recomposed by the light. The fountain is not playing. The water lies flat, eye-baffling marble-slab smooth or fountain-basin transparent. I like the idea of the place. Here, I can personally pass the brink at any moment, touched by the beauty of the site and the turmoil of a deceitful world revived in me like an instinct of which I would not be ashamed, that would fan to flames all my flammable thoughts. In this city I could write. Here, I exist.

I like the idea of the place. The fountain gives off a strong damp smell that reminds one of the tropics. A strange sensation amid the murmur of the water mingled with the clatter of tableware and echoing voices from the Café des Courbes. A seventeenth-century sculpture representing Amphitrite, wife of Poseidon, adorns the fountain's east side. This noisy site harbours a visual silence. I dare not move. Time comes my way, fountains of the entire world. I am energy, aura, a golden opportunity to meld with the idea of the place, with the water's trickling, whose significance suddenly becomes clear.

Tonight I aim to talk. About the sea. The translator is all ears. A fine opportunity. There isn't anything to interrupt me. In English, I tell her about the beach, the sand from which the child once gathered nautilus, clam and trumpet shells. The child stares into the sea's maw. The wind whips up a spindrift that makes miraculous rainbows and spray in the eyes. The child is learning new Greek and Latin words. She asks where the waves come from and why each always comes with a roar. The wind slicks her hair. The child rolls in time, then climbs astride the wind *travelling among questions. Aiming for the future.*

I leaf through a magazine featuring the chaos theory. Some fractals in colour. I'm stunned by the resemblance between fractals and psychedelic images. The telephone rings. The photographer. "I have a proposal for you." The first book under her imprint. She mentions an artist whose name I don't really catch. I could drop by the Dazibao Gallery to have a look. Later in the day: this woman does indeed produce images that go straight to the gut and light up the past, restoring it in composition virtual and fictional.

We walk for a long time on the pretext that rain in a civilized city excites one's sensuality. Tonight our bodies want to be free, unsheltered, unprotected. Crave excitement, sensations, liberating projections and city lights. Our bodies have ordered a good time tonight.

We come back to the future. Rain scudding over our cheeks. Right or wrong, we associate freedom and future as if the words made a morally compatible couple. And time-proof. We can't stop thinking future. The translator runs a hand through her hair, which is black and beautiful and glistens in the darkness.

I say, "How can we tell the difference between suffering with cause and suffering without cause?" The journalist makes a face. I continue: "We spend several hours a day entertaining ourselves with the suffering of others, without enjoying it for all that. Although we have it constantly before our eyes and know it's contemporary to our own lives, unthinkable suffering in others feeds our nightmares. It grabs the imagination and stirs up thoughts as does a work of art, a major theme that reinforces the precious convictions of our civilization. As early as 1925, you may recall, Valéry wrote, 'If there's no major catastrophe somewhere in the world this morning, we feel a certain emptiness.'" The journalist frowns and puts a final question, to which I reply with a quote from the photographer Diane Arbus: "One of the things I felt I suffered from as a kid was I never felt adversity. I was confirmed in a sense of unreality. And the sense of being immune was, ludicrous as it seems, a painful one." Then, softly, I conclude, "Yes, really, my cup runneth over."

We're sitting in the third row. From here I can make out everything: the mouth, a gathering of white saliva at the corner of the mouth, the drops of sputter, the hairs of the beard, the studied movements of the lips, eyebrows and chin, a hand preparing to clench into a fist, the mouth ready tā bark, "What was Baudelaire,/ what were Edgar Allan Poe, Nietzsche, Gérard de Nerval?/ **Bodies**/ that ingested/ digested/ rested/ snored at least once each night,/ shit 25 to 30,000 times,/ and stacked against 30 or 40,000 meals,/ 40 thousand sleeps,/ 40 thousand snores,/ 40 thousand sour, embittered mouths on waking,/ each have 50 poems to show for it,/ really it's not enough."[18]

At intermission we have a beer. In spite of the air-conditioning, the heat permeates every cranny of our bodies like a fine city soot penetrating our pores without our knowing.

"It's not an entertaining show."

"Why would it be? We're not here so we can forget we're here."

On Mount Royal. We talk about America at present and in the past. The translator recalls the distance covered by Cavelier de La Salle all the way to Louisiana. Colonies, districts, provinces, *départements*. Possessions and territories. Empire. Ships. We return to the future and the way we came. We walk a while around Beaver Lake. Squirrels chase in circles the way they do in cartoons. I don't know why but I think of Lewis Carroll's mathematical formulas. There's something engaging about wanting to live in the future when all the language of the past dazzles us so, holds us back by the underside of our imaginations.

Here identity is a subject that makes people run on, whereas for me it's a source of meditation. As a child, while taking my bath I would often contemplate my motionless feet at the other end of the tub as if they were alien things, two little bits of humanity which weren't any part of me. I could stay like this for long periods, not moving a hair, observing the distance between me and humanity, almost orgasmic with "that's not me down there because I'm pure mind up here." Only an act of will, like moving a toe, could restore my integrity, return me to my species of flesh and the reality of bathwater gone cold.

On the terrace at the Café Cherrier, all this sun parches one's lips. How is one to know ahead of time if one would say a character has thin, sensual, full or downy lips; a prominent, receding, cleft, double or nutcracker chin; a hooked, button, aquiline, pointed, snub, crooked, flat or Grecian nose; large, bulging, oriental or deep-set eyes? How can one tell if one would say her skin is pink, white or tanned and, later in the story, soft or smooth as satin? How is one to venture beyond these things without knowing if one would say a woman is a character or my beloved?

In a Saint-Laurent Boulevard bookstore. I inquire about a large illustrated book that is supposed to be out in London today. The bookseller consults his computer and, not seeing anything corresponding to what I'm looking for, makes inquiries of a London bookstore by E-mail. *"Yes, it came out a few hours ago. It's a gorgeous book. You shouldn't wait to order."* While this has been going on, the translator has been turning the pages of a two-month-old magazine. At the back of the store, two women are living it up in real time, reading *The Lesbian Body.*

What do you think of when you say "our" literature? I think of all the shards of words and utopia that make death improbable and paradoxically so present I don't know where to begin. The angst or baroque exuberance side. I only know we have to reread, rub against the mentality of the past, get used to the notion that there are whole chapters that relate directly to us. "Our" literature is inseparable from Literature, an ultimate nostalgia valid also for the future. Because a few centuries from now we will still be around, wondering, trembling a bellyful with anxiety and enchantment, the intelligence of our tears as sole proof of our humanity. And what do you think now that you've said all this? I think we have to reread.

We prop our elbows on the table. We lean toward each other, groping for whatever will accommodate the other in our intentions. We discuss the projection of our lives and of the past in a present free of confidences. We draw closer by revealing as little as possible of ourselves, a paradox. It strengthens the attraction and effect of saying *tu,* and our faces become the more expressive. We are physically of the same mind about many ideas. Our thoughts overlap. Each is eager to discover the so-called intimate wishes of the other. Surrounded by questions and constellations, too much of everything lickety-split draws us close.

We agreed to meet at the Harbour Clock Pier to hear and relive among artefacts the story of the *Empress of Ireland,* which was swallowed by the river off Rimouski. The translator: down the generations, the image of the sinking resurfaces, as does the notion of navigation which, with the innumerable manoeuvres it makes possible, we associate inevitably with the universe, the sea and the cosmos, and the billions of cells that sow immoderation and a strong yen for deviance in us.

Later, beneath a present perfect sky we board a paddle-boat from which Montreal will appear ever-changing. As we leave the island and gain the expanse of the river, my feeling of pleasure is so strong that a yearning to write comes over me. Back at the hotel, I order food and drink. I write until *I don't write any more* sinks as naturally as could be into the past of unworthy thoughts.

As I turned the page, I fell on a badly written passage, which I read avidly without pause, fascinated by what must have been going on in the author's head. I have been trying for years to understand the "badly written passage" phenomenon, a sudden and monstrous deficiency between the intent and the expression. A miscalculation or perhaps a punishment inflicted by the author on herself to compensate the discomfort of not being there, of being inadequately there at the heart of the prodigious thing moving in her.

Sometimes when I've finished reading a novel I'll think about what might happen next in the story, a fantasy indulged in by a reader for whom fiction works only if fiction is smitten with its own horizon. I call this getting ahead of the heroine, or author as the case may be. An interplay of ending and superstitions. Ramification without end, a new opening.

What's to be understood if I say a woman makes me think? What's to be imagined if I say she gives me a lot to think about? Our stories are similar, blending sometimes to the point where we have to make over the beginning and the end, whenever we lose sight of them totally and are forced thereby to connect belonging and identity, outside the story line, by showing nobility and solidarity.

She asks what day one of the novel was like. "A feeling of loneliness mixed with strong May sunshine libido. I had spent the morning at the British Museum and bought two books by Samuel Beckett on the way home. At Cecil Court I read while having tea. Suddenly a yen for the vast and lavish. This was the first time I had felt such a thing: the yen without the urgency. No imperative, just certainty that I would never more cease to think about it."

Ensconced in the big overstuffed chairs in the hotel lobby, several men are talking to themselves. Their voices spew here and there like small sound pebbles in the huge lobby space. Elbows cocked, mouths jammed against handpieces, clutching their cellular phones for all they're worth, they emit and receive brief messages that excite the contemporary *ego*. They are all free, equal and occupied, and attached to the "spasm of life," which is perfectly normal. The rest, in silence like me, are watching the revolving door out of the corner of an eye and thinking about the evening to come, about the restaurant, about the morrow. There she is, dressed to the nines, a book under her arm. I rise to greet her with a kiss. We pounce on a subject of conversation. I think back to the time when all subjects were racy and full of tantalizing ellipses and added bonuses in thoughts that ruled out compromise. The bonuses kindled semantic fires on every side. There was enigma to be unravelled, light to be swallowed and each moment to be tasted, with surprise at the reign of so much life.

The translator says, "Since you arrived I've begun an article in which you seem often to be silent. Your silence haunts me. Palpable, almost flesh among the words I write." I wasn't going to reply but, yes, silence draws people together. It knits without our being the wiser. Desire. I wasn't going to throw her a line twenty-four hours before taking off for London. I wasn't going to put on a youthful air and soon be mistaking one body for another. I wasn't going to think about literature here and go crazy trying to solve some riddle about silence. I wasn't going to hunt for an answer in language and hand it to her gazing at her hungrily.

"Silence," she says, "as if you were scanning the invisible, studying the night, the day or, let's say, the arrow of time. You watch the thing streak away then turn round and head back to you doing loop-the-loops. Your silence is drinkable too, cheers!" The wine slips down my throat, caresses my palate, my mucous membranes waken, the wine slips down nicely, warming as it goes, in my body it's slow and succulent. The wine, the line, palaces, cities, things are confused, I know, I'm in the eye of the hurricane. Babylon, the Tigris, Tigre, the veins in her neck when she swallows. I'm gone. When I get back we're dogged by the present. The silence. The music. I mention Buenos Aires. We hop in a taxi. Watch Montreal go by, its brick, stones, curlicue staircases, terraces, churches. Saint-Laurent Boulevard, number 4848. A large room, dim lighting under which couples yes, that's the verb *bailar*. Elbows on a red tablecloth so long it touches our knees, tango after tango we absorb the present.

I agreed. It must have been one in the morning when we arrived at the casino on Île Notre-Dame. We move up and down the aisles lined with hundreds of slot machines. People walking around like beggars with their baskets of small change. A constant tinkle of coins falling higgledy-piggledy, illusions, the ring of good luck. *Beat you bet*. It's madness. It's democratic and grasping. Money rains on every hand. On the second floor, you play at being rich. You enter the fiction of chips and symbols. You bet on the future, chip after chip, you call a number, give a nod as signal: one card, twice over. No one laughs.

On the way home we feel frightfully free to immerse our-selves in the near future. Montreal scintillates, a great mauve tattoo between the night and the first rays of dawn. The taxi moves slowly like a short sentence. One single body to compound with the young light of day and the words shining in the translator's eyes. The light strews rose across the sky. Images abound. Our bodies change every day without our knowing. Does the nature of our thoughts change because the body grasps the meaning of life on other planes? Can the body pay attention to the colour of the dawn and to things universal at the same time, and let fiction roll as well? The questions are back again. What are we to look for in the silence of others, with eyes enticed by proximity and whirligig comparisons day vastating us? What are we to look for in the very desire for comparisons and closeness?

NOTES

1. Louise Labé: *Baise-moi, baise m'encore.*
2. Nicole Brossard: *m'ange moi vaste.*
3. Paul Chanel Malenfant.
4. Paul Chanel Malenfant.
5. Leonardo da Vinci.
6. Homer.
7. Arthur Schopenhauer
8. Ludwig Wittgenstein.
9. Holy Bible, Genesis 6, 13; King James, New American and New English Versions respectively.
10. Herman Melville
11. Gérard de Cortanze
12. Abba Rock Group
13. Lewis Carroll
14. Lewis Carroll
15. Chevalier & Gheerbrant, *Dictionnaire de symboles.*
16. Miguel Ángel Asturias.
17. Louky Bersianik.
18. Antonin Artaud.

AFTERWORD

With this, the third book by Nicole Brossard that I have
translated, I have rediscovered the pleasure of working with
an author who combines depth of thought, richness of imagination and beauty of language with a keen interest in translation as a bridge between two systems of thought and
expression. I am fortunate indeed to have had her enthusiastic
and unsparing cooperation, to a point where this translation
is the result of a truly collaborative effort.

It is rarely recognized outside the ranks of academic lin-
guists that French and English, although they share an alpha-
bet and have swapped vocabulary over centuries, do not
conceive reality in the same way. English is fundamentally
more concrete, French more abstract; English more synthetic,
French more analytical. This is in part no doubt because
French, derived directly from Latin, was first a written language, a language of scholars, whereas English, with its
nomadic Indo-European-via-Germanic roots, began as a
spoken language, a language of the people that dealt first and

foremost with practical, down-to-earth matters. Accordingly, the extraordinary power of French to convey abstract thought, if it is to register forcefully in English, may need to pass through a filter of concrete expressions. The English mind, when faced with relentless abstractions, tends to turn off if not allowed to touch terra firma occasionally.

A subtle manifestation of difference is that certain aspects of a word or expression are often implied in one language but not in the other; conversely, certain distinctions may be important in the one, but in the other, if spelled out, are fussy, unnecessary details because they are already implied. In the course of translation, implied aspects in the source language may need to be filled in in the target language. For example, a *fleuve* is a major, navigable river (bigger than a *rivière*) whose implied breadth, etc., although important in the context, may not be conveyed by the word "river" alone. In a more complex example, the phrase *les folles de la place* is translated here as "the Mothers of the Plaza de Mayo," partly because this is the recognizable term in English but also because the dedication and determination implied in *folles* in the context is absent or too weakly implied in any appropriate term available in English.

Curiously, English is more rigid than French when it comes to verb tenses. A French text may drift back and forth from present to past and back again in a single sequence, for example, where the same in English will leave the reader puzzled and probably irritated. With Nicole's agreement, the tensing in English has been made more consistent in one or two instances where the drift has no particular significance and would look like mere carelessness on the author's part.

In keeping with her themes of inconsistency, paradox, contrast, even contradiction, Nicole juxtaposes passages of considerable formality and erudition with others that are very vernacular, with illogical, non-sequential leaps as in most spontaneous human thought and speech, and with crudity, invented words and offbeat or obscure words and concepts. These things have been noted and taken into account in the translation.

Nicole likes to jolt or provoke the reader once in a while, but characteristically she makes her points in subtle, indirect ways, often through metaphor, word play or word association. With her poet's ear and eye, she also creates rhythms, sound plays and visual effects which are to be preserved in one way or another, and which occasionally may even take precedence over sense.

She understands well that in translation compromise is inevitable, and has been willing to contemplate almost any kind of adaptation in our search for solutions to the "untranslatable." Still, an adaptation must work in order to be valid; a forced adaptation is a bad solution. In instances of metaphor or word association where, for example, sense and certain sound plays mesh naturally in French but no compromise in English works to a satisfactory degree, we have had to settle for either sense or sound play. There have been opportunites for recouping some of the unavoidable losses, however, through an occasional, naturally occurring word play or metaphor in English where there is none in French; this is known in translation theory as "compensation." All such inclusions, all adaptations, indeed countless points large and small have been scrutinized, discussed, sometimes reworked, and finally agreed upon between us. Throughout, Nicole's intention has been the guide. Some solutions have been initiated by Nicole herself.

There have been some minor editorial corrections, for example, "fifteen metres" instead of fifty, which should have been fifteen in the first place. Some of the passages in italics were in English in the original French text.

I could not close without expressing my sincere thanks to Nicole for her unfailing generosity with her time, patience and commitment to this undertaking. I also wish to thank Jacqueline Beaudoin Ross of the McCord Museum of Canadian History, Jean-Marc Frédette of the Service de la faune du Gouvernement du Québec, and the Redpath Library and the Religious Studies Library, both of McGill University, for their assistance on certain terminological and other questions. Finally and indispensably, I wish to thank Margaret McClintock and the late Coach House Press for their steadfast faith and encouragement throughout a large part of this project, as well as Ellen Seligman at McClelland & Stewart, who picked up the ball, so to speak, and, with enthusiasm and many astute observations and suggestions, has brought the project to fruition.

Patricia Claxton
February 1997